# Ellen

# Ellen

## ITA DALY

POOLBEG

First published in 1986 by Jonathan Cape Ltd
Black Swan edition published 1987

This edition published 1995 by
Poolbeg Press Ltd
Knocksedan House,
123 Baldoyle Industrial Estate,
Dublin 13, Ireland

The Publishers gratefully acknowledge the support of
The Arts Council.

A catalogue record for this book is available from the British Library.

ISBN 1 85371 460 7

Cover illustration by Laura Cronin
Cover design by Poolbeg Group Services Ltd
Printed by The Guernsey Press Ltd,
Vale, Guernsey, Channel Islands.

*For David*

# 1

I don't know why I was an only child, and certainly I have never asked my parents for an explanation. I do know that it placed a burden on me, turning me into an oddity when I might otherwise have been an ordinary little girl starting out at school. In the terrace where we lived, with its dank front gardens and aggressively shining door-knockers, I was a phenomenon; entire football teams emerged from our road, and its mean, uncurved length teemed with prams and broken toys and bread-and-jam-smeared children of all ages. I used to watch the mothers, dragging children and shopping, glance slyly at our lace curtains. I could imagine them calculating – two whole bedrooms and a sitting-room and kitchen and scullery and only three people to fill it all. I wondered too where their seven or eight offspring were bedded down at night, but I was never friendly enough with any of them to find out.

As an only child I never felt indulged or cherished although I was conscious of my parents' unblinking attention.

'You'll end up with a BA after your name or it won't be my fault,' my mother would say before the ritual clearing of the tea table to make room for my homework. Later, when I went to secondary school, she bought me a desk and one-bar electric fire so that I might study undisturbed in my own bedroom. That fire was to become the symbol of her unfulfilled and foolish hopes. When she had been made to realize, finally, that having failed my Leaving Certificate I might not even enter university, she took the fire and hurled it in the glory-hole under the stairs. It remained there until the February that she died, when my father, remembering its existence, plugged it in at the bottom of her bed in an effort to melt the ice in her big, buniony feet.

Mother washed her hands of me. 'I don't care,' she said to father. 'I don't care what she does. Let her get a job cleaning the streets for all I care. So long as she doesn't go and take the mail boat to England and bring further disgrace on us all.'

Within a fortnight my father had found me a job. 'Didn't you do some typing at school? Well then, Jack Taylor has decided he needs a secretary and you can start next Monday.'

Jack Taylor was one of father's friends. Father's friends never came to the house and he never went to theirs. I had often doubted their existence in the past and it seemed ironic that I should be rescued now by one of them.

Jack was a shy and retreating boss. He worked in the back room, sawing and gluing, fitting holy pictures into frames. I kept the books, made the tea, typed the odd few letters. At lunch time I made more tea and we ate our sandwiches in separate rooms. I think he was as terrified of me as I was of him. If he wanted to use the lavatory in the back yard, instead of going out the back door which opened off my office, he walked out the front door, down to the corner and up the back lane where he tiptoed through the back entrance to the little shed. I myself never visited the shed until he left his workroom, for I knew that his workbench was facing a large window which looked out on the back yard. Now I realized that our joint delicacy could have led to the situation in which we both met up at the shed door together, having approached it from different ends. I blushed at the very thought of such embarrassment and promised myself to drink less tea.

The office was small and dark and most of the time I managed to feel invisible. Clients, when they called, had to peer at me through the gloom, and anyway my body was obscured by the high, old-fashioned typewriter and the kitchen table on which it sat.

'Don't you get lonely sometimes, with just yourself and Jack?'

My mother had forgiven me and had started taking an interest in my life again.

'No, I don't get lonely.'

'And you never go out in the evenings. Now that you've no studying to do, Ellen, you should get out a bit more, think about enjoying yourself. And I've been meaning to talk to you about your clothes – you really should get some new ones. I mean, you really can't create a good impression, wearing those old things you've had since school. You need to look smart now that you're at business.'

'Jack doesn't care how I look.'

'Don't you believe that, my girl, all men like a girl to look nice. And you must admit, Ellen, you don't even try. You've got lovely eyes. You should wear more blue, bring them out.'

I could see what was happening. This was her new fantasy – I was going to be a social success, even if I had failed scholastically.

'I'm going upstairs to clean my shoes for the morning.'

'Good girl, neatness is half the battle. And Ellen,' she followed me into the hall, 'why don't you bring some of your friends home some evening? Bring someone round for tea, they'd be more than welcome.'

I had never brought a friend home because I *had* no friend. We had never been part of the easy intercourse of the terrace, mother considering herself a cut above the rest, and the rest, naturally, resenting this. So while other children played, I sat inside and looked out through the lace curtains. At school, shy and snarling and sniffing patronage in every offer of friendship, I was eventually left alone. And when I was, I felt the sour triumph of vindication – my assessment of myself as ugly and worthless had been proved right. Now, my

9

isolation seemed normal, I was used to being on my own. And with the humiliations of school behind me, I could even say as I shuffled around in the perpetual twilight of that wet November, my first winter as a working girl, that I was content. Inside my navy nap school coat my inviolability seemed complete. But I dreaded the winter equinox when the days would begin to get longer and I would have to walk the length of the city streets uncamouflaged.

'What's the light doing on in the front room?'

Father broke the silence. I had bumped into him as he was getting off the bus from work and we had walked home together. I liked father but we embarrassed one another. I raised my head now to follow his pointing finger. Light from our front room shone through the thin curtains, the only house showing illumination in the whole length of the terrace. Ours was an economical neighbourhood where people lived in back kitchens and lights were switched off in halls.

'Was your mother expecting anyone?'

'Not that I know.'

But I guessed why the sitting-room was lit up. For more than a fortnight now mother had been threatening to take my social life in hand, to end my moping, as she put it.

In stealth we sidled up the tiny garden path.

'I'll just pop up and change these shoes,' whispered father, eyeing with alarm the green tweed coat on the hall-stand.

'So there you are!' Mother had the stance of battle in her thrusting chest. 'Come in both of you and see who's here.'

The girl by the fire smiled with insouciance. From the door I could see the cracks in the red paint of her mouth.

'It's Cissie Brennan's little girl – little Celia.' Mother sounded as if she had just produced a rabbit from a hat and little Celia smiled on.

'You remember what friends Ellen and Celia were

10

when the Brennans lived here. Mrs Brennan and I used to say they were like Siamese twins. I thought what a good idea it would be if we all got together again. It's such a pity to lose touch.'

Celia tried to hide a yawn. Father and I stared at her in silence.

'Well, Tom,' mother prodded, 'did you ever think you'd see Celia Brennan looking so elegant, here in our sitting-room?'

Father cleared his throat. 'How's your mother keeping then?'

'Fine, Mr Yates.'

'And your father?'

'Oh, tip-top form.'

Father rocked back on his heels. The fire roared up the chimney, already overpowering the dimensions of the tiny room.

'Well then,' mother began to back towards the door as if she were withdrawing from royalty, 'I'll just go and see how things are getting on.' I began to shuffle after her but she put up a hand. 'No, no – you young people stay and have a chat. Tom is very useful in the kitchen.'

There was no escape. I moved to an upright chair and sat, my back to the wall. Celia had taken out a packet of twenty Churchmans.

'Smoke?'

I shook my head, wishing I could say yes and covertly watching the elegance of the ritual.

'Damn.' Celia extended her middle finger for my inspection. 'Isn't that just the most annoying thing? It's taken me weeks to grow them all to this length and I've been so careful, wearing rubber gloves all the time. Doesn't it drive you mad when this happens?'

I pressed my pink and nibbled quicks more firmly into my armpits and wondered if she expected an answer.

Celia yawned again, looking around the room with frank interest. 'It's nice here, isn't it? I can hardly remember living next door but I do remember that I always liked it. I used to think it so cosy.' She patted the

11

plasterboard behind her and it echoed hollowly. 'Of course Mam always wanted something bigger, that's really why we moved. But it suits you fine, doesn't it, with only the three of you?'

Her eyes had come to rest on me with a sort of mild curiosity. I blushed at the image I must present – haunches spreading inside blue serge, ankles bulging over flat school shoes. Why was mother determined to persecute me? Why couldn't she just let me be?

'Ooh, it is hot.' Celia began to push back the chair with petulant and ineffective shoves. I remained seated. 'Of course, I'm not used to open fires. We have the central heating at home. A fire is nice but don't you find it very dirty?'

'I think I'd better go and see if I can give a hand.'

I realized when I had said the words that they were the first I had spoken, yet it felt as if I had spent an entire day in her company.

'Okey-doke.' She took out a compact and began to examine her face. 'I hate to seem rude but I'll have to be off quite early. I explained it all to your mother before you came in . . .' She threw her eyes heavenwards and offered me a knowing smile to share. 'The boyfriend! Have to meet him every single night when he's finished studying. He's at the Uni. Your mother was very decent about it when I explained – said we'd be finished tea in plenty of time.'

The kitchen table could not hold all the food and the overflow was arranged on a card table by the window.

'We'll never eat all that.'

Mother smiled complacently. 'I'd prefer it said that you got too much food in my house than too little. Now, go and get the girl – no, let your father do it. You start folding these serviettes, I got pink ones to match the tablecloth. Don't they just set it off?'

Mother squeezed me in between the card table and Celia. Our elbows kept on bumping and Celia kept on saying pardon. Mother had placed the alarm clock on a shelf on the dresser so that we might all share the responsibility of getting Celia off on time. Its tinny tick-tock accentuated the silences which, despite mother's efforts, fell more heavily with every sausage roll we ate. Celia seemed quite overcome by the feast. I watched her wilt, hair growing lank, her make-up ridging in minia-ture hills around her nose. Of course, being used to central heating she probably found our range a bit much, with mother jumping up every few minutes to stuff another sod of turf down its gullet.

'Well now, this *has* been nice,' mother said as we stood in the hall and watched Celia renewing her make-up. 'You must call again Celia, love. Or maybe Ellen could go round and see you. It would be nice for her to see your mother after all these years.'

'Oh we'll get together, never you fear.' Celia had perked up now that escape was imminent. 'And thank you for the lovely spread, Mrs Yates – you really shouldn't have gone to so much trouble.'

'Trouble? It was a pleasure. Now, off you go, Tom will see you to the bus. I don't want that boyfriend of yours blaming me for keeping you late.'

We had finished the washing-up by the time father returned. Mother hadn't spoken to me except to remark that when she went to the trouble of entertaining my friends the least I could do was let it be seen that I had a tongue in my head.

'That Celia's a grand little girl.' Father's tone was one of appeasement.

Mother grunted. 'She makes the most of herself, I'll give her that. But poor thing, she's no oil painting now, is she? I've always hated brown eyes, they're so dead in the head. And that nose. But as I've always said – you don't need to be Betty Grable to get a boyfriend. Celia has a nice friendly manner and a smile for the world and that goes a long way.'

She didn't have to look at me, I knew quite well for whom she intended those remarks. But couldn't she understand that it wasn't wilfulness that made me dull

13

and ugly? No amount of smiling was going to turn me into a Celia any more than desks and electric fires had made me a scholar. I felt sorry for her, stuck with me for a daughter. But I should have realized that she wasn't beaten yet, that she was still determined to provide me with friends and what she saw as a normal life.

Often now when I returned home from work there would be some unknown girl seated on our tweed settee in the front room. Always a different one, always a stranger.

Father asked me whether I thought she might have put an ad in the evening paper, and certainly I was amazed that she could find so many victims. Some of them were cousins, others were the daughters and nieces of old friends. I had found her one evening, sitting at the table, leafing through the pages of a tattered diary. It had 1940, the year I was born, embossed in faded gold letters on the cover. Inside there was nothing but names and addresses, as far as I could see. Her social life must have stopped soon after that, overwhelmed by the demands of motherhood. And now she was dredging up all these old acquaintances so that I might have friends. I was sorry for her but I was terrified for myself. The house began to have the air of an hotel, strange coats in the hall, strange voices in the sitting-room. I reached the stage of total speechlessness and father assumed a hunted look, but mother still persisted. The guest, puzzled as to why she had been asked, would sit through the abundant meal and disappear for ever from our lives. Mother's suggestions – another visit, a little outing for the girls – were never taken up but she did not despair. As I approached home on these evenings I would feel the nausea rising in my throat.

One night, I couldn't take it any more. As I rounded the corner and saw our front room window lit up for the second time that week, I turned and walked back the way I had come.

I had no plan, just the instinct to escape. The night was damp and greasy. As I passed a chip shop on the

14

main road, saliva filled my mouth at the smell, a mixture of frying fat and vinegar. I wished I had the courage to go in, even to stand at the counter and take a packet of chips out with me. I turned up the collar of my coat and shuffled on, trying to ignore the hunger pangs. At first I felt uneasy, with the darkness, the clamminess of my skin in the damp air. As I walked, however, my spirits began to lift. Most people had gone home for tea and the empty streets were different, balmy and without threat. I found myself looking up instead of down as I usually did, and as the tension left my muscles I felt a surge of freedom. The lemon street lamps threw lozenges of light, just enough to guide me from one to the next. The old tenement houses on either side soared like cathedrals and I was heady in the sudden rush of space. Occasionally I caught angled glimpses of interiors, the outline of a head, a flowered plastic shade. Passing one house, a window flew open and a woman's voice said, 'Could you tell us the time, love? All the clocks in this house is stopped.'

My answer echoed down in the dark area where small things scuttled.

I don't know how far I walked. Sometimes I felt myself lost and then, turning a corner, would find myself up against a dairy or sweet shop I had known all my life. After a while there were a few more people about, on bicycles, freewheeling towards town, in buses, fussing past. I didn't mind them though, mere bobbing outlines in the friendly dark. I felt I could keep this up all night, infected as I was by the magic of this downy, anonymous city. Then I passed a cinema with people coming out and I realized it must be after ten. There would be hell to pay at home.

Father was waiting at the end of our road and I could see mother at the garden gate, light streaming out from the open door behind her.

'We thought you'd had an accident,' he said, touching my arm awkwardly. 'I was just on my way to Jack's to see if he knew anything. Your poor mother's in an awful state.'

15

She stood weeping and thrusting her hands into her ribcage as if trying to stop her heart from popping out. 'How could you,' her voice was piteous. 'How could you do this to us!'

'I'm sorry, I didn't –'

'What did we ever do to you to make us suffer like this?'

'It wasn't –'

'And where have you been, Miss? What have you been doing out till this hour of the night? No respectable girl walks in unaccompanied at such a time. Where have you been?'

I could see that there was no point in offering the truth; even to me it sounded unconvincing.

'Well, Miss? I'm waiting.'

'I met a friend. We had tea in a hotel.' I thought this touch might mollify her.

'A likely story.' She turned into the house and we followed. 'Put the kettle on, Tom, I won't sleep a wink anyway so I might as well have a cup of tea. Well?' She faced me. 'And who is this friend that you happened to meet so mysteriously? I must say I find it a little strange that we've never heard of her before.'

'It's because she was away. She's been staying with her grandmother in –' I searched round desperately for an Irish county – 'in Cork.'

Mother's expression remained sceptical.

'We were at school together and the coincidence is that I bumped into her just at the convent gates. I'm sorry I was so late back, but we had so much to chat about and once we got into the hotel lounge it was so comfortable there that I just forgot the time.'

I was amazed at the fluency of my lies. 'I'm meeting her again next week. She really is a very nice girl and she was saying how great it was to meet someone from school, that she's lost touch with the others.'

Mother had begun to smile. 'Come,' she said, patting the chair beside her at the table, 'come and have something to eat. Hotels may be comfortable but I've never

16

known them to be generous in the food line. Now – tell me all about this friend, what's her name? Did I ever meet her at the school dos? I've such a bad memory for faces but I'm good on names.'

I came to regret my inventiveness. It *had* put a stop to the tea parties but it also meant that I was stuck with my new friend. If I were to kill her off or send her packing back to her grandmother in County Cork, I knew that mother would start searching for a replacement with renewed vigour. By now she had a name (Hilary O'Herlihy – I liked the ring of it), and an address and a family; she also suffered from a debilitating shyness, which kept her out of mother's reach. I quite enjoyed inventing a life for her and I enjoyed the freedom which her existence had conferred on me. For a month, six weeks, I ranged happily through the city streets, winter streets, deserted. I became more daring and ventured into unknown neighbourhoods. Sometimes I would take a posh walk through roads where houses were semi-detached and winter roses grew on long, sad stems. Sometimes I would find pockets of real poverty which made our terrace seem quite grand. But now I had begun to notice a sudden lengthening of the day.

A fortnight ago I had walked, unselfconsciously, in the woolly dark. Now the light refused to go but got brighter and brasher with every passing night. The weather grew less dank and there were more people about. Everywhere there was noise and movement and girls in pale cardigans swinging tennis rackets. I would cross the street to avoid them but was struck with sudden longing for a real friend. I listened as their chatter faded and imagined what it must be like to walk along arm-in-arm with someone else.

There were sudden showers in April and as I stood on the steps of the public library, sheltering from one of them, I thought that I had better buy an umbrella.

'I'm sorry, but I'm going to have to close these.'

I turned to see a girl with a bunch of keys in her hand

17

standing just behind me. She was pointing towards the doors of the library, one of which I was leaning against. I blushed with the guilty feeling that I had no right to be standing there, and was slinking off when she called me back.

'Could you give me a hand, these doors are so heavy.'

We grasped a brass knob each and pulled the doors to. I had turned away for a second time when she stopped me again. 'I'm sorry to deprive you of your shelter but I had to lock up. Haven't you got an umbrella – it's lashing.'

Overcome by my own foolishness, I blushed again.

'Here, we can share mine, you'll get soaked if you head off in this. I just live round the corner, so if you like you can walk me home and then I'll give you the umbrella.'

As she was talking she had begun to open a pink umbrella. Now she thrust it at me. 'You'd better hold it, you're taller than me. Come on, we'll both get pneumonia if we hang around here.'

She took my arm and nudged me forward. 'They said on the weather forecast this morning that it was going to be fine – that's why I brought my brolly. I always do the opposite to what they say; if you do that you won't be caught out.'

I could feel her arm in mine, I could feel the length of her body and her breath on my hand. She chattered and I turned my face to listen but didn't hear. I walked entranced throuh the rain, overwhelmed by the little creature at my side, her ease and warmth. I didn't have a chance to feel shy or self-conscious. I was being talked at, smiled on, nudged as if I had known her all my life. This was the friend I had never had, even if she only lasted to the end of the street. Gratitude swelled in me for I knew by the way she looked at me, by the confiding tone of the unintelligible words, that I was being treated as a peer, an ordinary girl, even a potential pal.

She stopped in front of a brown-painted door.

'What will I do with the umbrella?' I asked.

'It doesn't matter. Leave it in the library sometime you're passing, I have another if I'm stuck.'

The casualness of her voice made me blush at my presumptions.

'Listen – I've got a better idea. Why don't you bring it round tomorrow about six? It's my early evening – maybe we could have a cup of coffee or something afterwards. Unless you're busy tomorrow.'

I jumped over puddles on the way home and then began to count the lines in the pavement – anything to block out what had happened. If I allowed myself to think about it, I might wake up and discover that I had been dreaming. Anyway, I must keep a hold on myself. A cup of coffee was no commitment to friendship. Tomorrow night she was bound to find me out, my dullness, my other inadequacies. It wasn't very likely that I would see her again after that.

But I couldn't stop my heart from singing as I raced home. I turned my face upwards and licked the rain that fell on my lips. It tasted of smoke and was unexpectedly cold. I might join the library, become a reader like father, although he only ever read paperbacks which he picked up on the Quays. I could ask her how you joined and other questions. Mother said that a good conversationalist always showed interest in the other person. Tonight, before I went to bed, I could make out a list of questions that I could ask about the library.

I had a Best Friend. Best Friends went for walks together, supported one another, had laughs and chats together in the evenings over cups of coffee and tea. Best Friends also quarrelled, but not us, never us. If Myra asked me to cut off my hand, I would close my eyes and chop it off – I was quite sure of that. I was her shadow; I smiled when she smiled and sighed when she sighed. To have a friend of my own was miraculous enough, but to have such a friend . . . I watched her now across the table, her prettiness, her vitality, like a glow in the smoky café.

19

She smiled at me and I looked away in case she might see the extravagance of my emotion. I must pretend casualness, never frighten her off.

'Hey.'

'What?'

'I asked you a question – you don't listen, Ellen. *Have* you ever thought of leaving home?'

'No.' My answer was easy for I knew it couldn't be a serious question.

'Why not?'

'Because.'

'No, I'm serious. Have you never thought of moving into a flat? I mean, don't you ever feel you'd like more independence, not have somebody telling you what to do all the time?'

I had never thought of leaving home, city girls didn't. If you came from the country and had to work in town then you had to live either in a flat or digs, like Myra. But a city girl stayed at home until she got married, or unless she was put out for disgracing her family in some way. And anyway, I didn't mind living at home. Before I had met Myra I would have been unhappy anywhere; now, I couldn't imagine myself more content.

'It's all right, living at home. I mean, I don't mind it.'

'I couldn't bear it. I couldn't bear being treated like a child all the time or having nowhere to entertain my friends.'

I didn't point out that she had nowhere to entertain her friends now.

'And I think it's good for you. It stands to reason that you only mature when you're out on your own.'

I admitted to myself that there was probably some truth there.

'Would you?'

'Would I what?'

'Leave home. Share a flat with me.'

But . . . hadn't it merely been a disinterested conversation then? It had never occurred to me, I had never even thought – she had never complained about her digs. But I couldn't. I stopped there, not allowing myself to think past the fact that I knew I couldn't. Mother would be even more upset than when I had failed my Leaving Certificate, she would see it as a rejection of herself. And she didn't even like Myra. She said she sounded uppity, but I think the truth was that she resented my secrecy. I had talked endlessly of Hilary, sharing our imaginary adventures with mother, but Myra I kept to myself.

'Wouldn't it be fun to share a flat – wouldn't it, Ellen? Think of it, the things we could do. And you must admit we get on very well together.'

I had to gather all my courage to oppose her. I was afraid of standing up to her and, anyway, I *wanted* to give her what she liked. Only I couldn't this time, not with mother to be faced.

'I couldn't Myra, Mammy would have a fit.'

'Mammy this, Mammy that – you're such a baby.'

I stared into my cup. This was it, our first quarrel.

'And stop sulking now, I hate people who sulk.'

'I'm sorry Myra, really I am, but I just couldn't do it. Nobody leaves home when they have a family in the city, they just don't. I mean, they'd have no reason.'

'Sometimes you can be really stupid. Oh, come on – let's forget it. You look as if you're going to start crying. Here, have another coffee.'

'Is it all right if I go to Sligo next week-end? The Bolands have invited me.'

Mother sniffed. 'I never knew you were so disloyal, Ellen, I never would have believed it till now. A month ago it was Hilary here and Hilary there. Now you've no time for anyone but that Boland lady.'

'But I've told you – Hilary had to go back to her grandmother's, she's living in Cork again.'

'Of course you wouldn't think of visiting there. Not good enough for you, I suppose.'

'I wasn't invited.'

Mother sniffed again and turned towards the window.

21

'No need to ask me if you can go to Sligo, it's your own business. Once you're earning your own living parents have little say.' She continued to stare out the window into the little yard where the kitchen chairs were piled up, waiting to be scrubbed. Then she relented.

'I'd advise you to take your best underwear – you can have my American nightie if you like. You can laugh now but you'd be amazed how much confidence a bit of lace will give you when you're faced with all them mahogany chests of drawers.'

We shared a carriage with a woman who offered us boiled sweets, great for travel sickness she said. Then a man got in and Myra nudged me. 'Just my type,' she mumured behind her hand.

He looked old to me.

As the train began to heave itself out of the gloomy station, I could feel the excitement in my belly. Sligo, Cairo, it was all the same to me. Being the child of Dublin parents, I had never travelled on country holidays. Suburban trains to the seaside were the only ones I knew. This was a proper train with a ticket collector and a dining-car. Myra said that we might have tea there later on.

'I hate this journey,' Myra told me as she set up a game of patience on the seat between us. 'It reminds me of going back to school. You've no idea how much I hated my boarding school.'

The woman opposite had taken out her knitting; the man was nodding off. I opened a magazine and pretended to read. It would take three hours to complete the journey to Sligo.

The streets of Sligo were narrow with high houses. In the sunshine the town wore a run-down air. Because it was Saturday afternoon it was crowded with country people doing their weekly shopping. They chatted outside doorways, resting on bicycles, shopping bags and brown paper parcels at their feet. We walked along the gutter, steering a course between traffic and gossipers. When we reached a square Myra said, 'We live over there,' and pointed across.

The square seemed quiet after the bustle of the street. In the middle there was a statue of a man with a gun, kneeling, ready to shoot. At its base, cars were parked, higgledy-piggledy. Before an open door two children were hunkered down, chalking the pavement. Absorbed, they didn't notice us until Myra called out, 'Hugh, Rose.' Then they were up and flinging themselves at her. 'We've been waiting for hours,' the little girl said. 'We thought you were never coming.'

They grabbed our bags and staggered up some steps and in through the open door. In the hallway I noticed an odd smell, cold and pungent.

'Where's Mam?'

'Doing her hair.'

'I might have known. Did you smell the peroxide, Ellen? Is Dad in?'

'Down in the surgery. What did you bring us?'

'Later. Come on, Ellen, we'd better go and let Mam know we've arrived.'

We mounted the stairs and the smell grew stronger. On the return, Myra banged on a door. 'Mam, we're here.'

The door was opened and a woman peered out. She stared and then fell back in theatrical horror. 'But I didn't expect you for hours.'

She was holding a toothbrush in one hand and I noticed that her hair, caught up in bunches like a school-girl's, was more brilliantly golden on one side than the other. She was wearing what I thought of as a kimono – certainly it was much too glamorous to be described as a dressing-gown.

'I've been doing my hair,' she said unnecessarily, 'the fumes are probably all over the house.' She turned to look at herself in the mirror and then came forward with outstretched hands. She smiled at me and I got a shock as I saw the brown stains on her teeth. 'How did you

23

arrive? I really didn't expect you for hours.'

'Then you're stupid. You should know that there's only one train on a Saturday. Are the beds ready at least?'

I waited for some reaction to her daughter's rudeness but Mrs Boland didn't seem to mind. She put her arm around my shoulder and smiled at me again. 'She's an awful fuss-pot, this daughter of mine, isn't she, Ellen? And we're so pleased you could come, Ellen, we've heard so much about you. Now, I want you to have a nice, relaxed week-end. Do exactly what you want – stay in bed for the two days if you feel like it. And don't let Myra bully you into doing anything you don't want to.' Then her expression became abstracted and she seemed to lose interest in me as she began to dab at her hair with the toothbrush.

'Come on.' Myra grabbed my arm, leading me up another flight of stairs. 'Mam is just impossible, she gets everything mixed up. Here, you're sleeping in here. At least I see she made the bed.'

My bedroom was enormous and smelled of stale perfume and mothballs. There was dust everywhere, inches thick, but I was touched by a little jug of flowers on the bedside table. Mother had been right about the mahogany chests of drawers – there were three of them and a wardrobe like a butcher's cold room. Inside there were clothes hangers, covered in velvet, and a china chamber pot. I wondered, with a blush, if I were supposed to use it. For all I knew, flush toilets had not yet arrived in Sligo.

I had finished putting my clothes away, with mother's good nightie under my pillow, when Myra came back. She was frowning and she beckoned me impatiently from the doorway.

'Come on, that woman hasn't bought a thing for tomorrow's dinner. We'll have to hurry or the butcher's will be closed.'

We bought meat and potatoes and two packets of raspberry jelly. Myra hurried me from shop to shop, ignoring the greetings of the shopkeepers, and made straight for the kitchen when we got home. 'I'll have to get the tea – nobody else will think of it.' She stood in front of the Aga and started throwing sausages and black pudding onto a cast-iron frying pan. The little ones grizzled at the table and smoke rose upwards from the burning fat.

'What on earth are you doing?' Mrs Boland appeared at the kitchen door. Her hair was now held up with combs and she wore a red dress.

'What does it look like?' Myra didn't bother to turn round.

'You haven't met Ned,' Mrs Boland said to me, producing a little man from behind her back. He had Myra's dark curls and bright brown eyes.

'How do,' he said, and took a gulp of whiskey from the glass in his hand. Then, as an afterthought, 'Would you care for a drink?'

Mrs Boland answered for me. 'Don't be silly, Ned, Ellen's just out of school.' He looked at me disbelievingly and then with a shrug turned round.

'See you later.' Mrs Boland blew us a kiss. 'Be good now.'

The smells of whiskey and perfume mingled with that of the frying pork.

'Here.' Myra banged plates down on the table. 'I think the only time they want me down here is when the maid walks out. I come in quite handy then.' Her face brightened. 'Would you like a glass of sherry, Ellen? I'm sure there's a bottle upstairs somewhere. How about it? We'll get these little ones off to bed and then we can have a nice evening by ourselves. The parents won't be back before eleven.'

'But wouldn't they mind? Your mother said just now –'

'They won't know. Sherry wouldn't be strong enough for that pair. Just wait here while I go and root it out.'

The rest of the week-end passed with a sense of mounting unreality. On Sunday morning I experienced my first hangover and the curious state of detachment that goes with it. The echoing darkness of the house, the heat of the square, the unexplained entrances and exits of Myra's family imbued the atmosphere with a theatricality which enchanted me. I could have sat in these stalls for ever.

Sunday lunch had the appearance of reality to begin with. We sat round the linen-covered dining-room table while Dr Boland stood at the head, making ready to carve. This was how I had imagined it would be. The first shock was the food. It was not that it was bad, it was inedible. The mutton seemed to be all fat and gristle and I could not get my knife through it. I noticed the little ones lifting lumps of it in their fists and gnawing – obviously the only manner of tackling it. The cabbage was a brilliant green but tasted strongly of bread-soda and the potatoes were parboiled. When the phone rang, Mrs Boland went to answer it. She came back, beaming. 'A call, Ned, old Sean Hogan out in Drumcliffe. I'll drive you.' And they scampered from the dining-room like Victorian children from a stern nanny.

They brought us to the station that evening and deposited us with kisses and presents, country eggs and a half fruit cake each, baked by Sean Hogan's wife. How beautiful Mrs Boland looked, despite her stained teeth, as she stood on the platform. She was wearing a green woolly suit and she held up the collar with one white hand and shivered, although I didn't think it cold. The children clung to her and I thought how bereft a little group they appeared, as if their mainstay had been taken away from them.

'Come and visit us again soon,' they called. 'Make it soon.'

I was in love. If Myra's parents had been ordinary I would still have been bowled over by a house where there were real paintings on the walls and where the biscuits were kept in a barrel. But Myra's parents were creatures of glamour, more like people in a magazine

26

story than those who inhabited my Dublin world. And that they should know my name, that they should have invited me back to their house made me weepy with gratitude.

'I really do like your family,' I offered timidly as Myra and I sat in the empty carriage on our way back to Dublin.

'Do you?' Myra yawned. 'Sometimes I wish they'd grow up a bit. Anyway, I got what I wanted so the visit wasn't entirely wasted.'

I hadn't realized that there had been a purpose behind our visit.

'Dad's going to write to your parents to ask them if they would let you share a flat with me. He promised he'd write tonight before he forgets.'

The train whistle shrilled and we plunged into a tunnel. In the darkness I was aware of a sudden chill. Myra was my entire world, I would do anything for her, but now, in this darkened carriage, I felt a stab of resentment against her. She had no right to behave as she had, and without even a word to me. It was the sneakiness of her plan that I found most upsetting, and as we re-entered the world of daylight, I looked at her bland, smiling face and for the first time found nothing there to admire.

'You're not cross with me?'

I didn't answer.

'Ah, come on, Ellen. I know you're afraid of what your mother will say but you can always blame me. It'll all blow over before you know it – and think of the fun we'll have together. There were other girls I could have asked to share, Ellen, but you're my best friend. If I couldn't share with you, I wasn't interested. Come on now, Ellen – what do you say? I should have told you but I knew you'd never agree. Will you forgive me?' She reached over and squeezed my hand. 'Friends?'

Then I realized that there was nothing to forgive.

'So, I suppose it was all four course meals and linen serviettes.'

Mother was black-leading the range when I returned,

27

an unusual task for a Sunday evening. I noticed too that the house had been spring-cleaned in my absence; the lace curtains and antimacassars were stiff with starch.

'It wasn't a bit like that.'

'I'm sure.'

'It wasn't . They aren't like that at all. Mrs Boland is very easy-going. I don't think she worries very much about housework.'

Mother stared at me speculatively. 'Paints her nails I suppose.'

'What's wrong with that?'

'And I wouldn't be surprised if she dyes her hair too. That's the other sort, much worse.'

'At least she's not dull and boring and worried all the time about what the neighbours think.'

I ran from the kitchen before mother could reply, exhilarated by my defiance. I was answering back like a normal daughter, giving cheek, as other girls of my age did. Myra was right, I was old enough not to be afraid of my mother any more, I should be standing up for myself, giving my opinions.

Then I thought of the letter, soon on its way from Sligo, and my boldness evaporated. She'd murder me.

Every morning I listened for the sound of a letter falling on the polished linoleum in the hall. We seldom got letters, except at Christmas, so on Wednesday I knew this was it when the letter-box snapped to. Ten seconds, I counted, the letter is picked up, back to the kitchen, five seconds, door closes, ten seconds. Then it came.

'Tom!'

Mother's shriek made me jump though I had been waiting for it.

'Jesus, Tom, come here at once.'

When the kitchen door had closed on both of them, I slipped out of the house.

All through the day my stomach heaved and lurched at the thought of the forthcoming confrontation. Now that the issue had been forced, I was prepared to fight. I wanted to be out of that matchstick house where sounds carried from room to room, destroying even the pretence of privacy. I wanted to be away from my parents' concern, from the memory of their pity. Tonight I was going to make a stand, even if it was a shaky one.

And then, when I returned from work, mother wasn't there. I forced myself to walk calmly into the kitchen, only to find it empty. The table was laid for two, with cold meat waiting under an inverted plate. I looked for a note but found none. Did she intend to steal my thunder by being the first to leave home?

By the time my father returned I was worried. I could not remember her ever being absent for a meal. Even when she didn't eat, she was there, to attend to our needs.

'Wet the tea, girl,' father said, rolling up his cardigan sleeves as he sat down at the table. 'Never you worry, she's just a bit upset and needs to get out. And,' he waved his knife at me, 'you leave it all to me when she does come back.'

It seemed strange to be sitting there without her, as if she were dead and these were the funeral baked meats. The neatly ordered kitchen seemed disarrayed; the row of saucepans above the gas stove shone less brightly in her absence. I sensed, with surprise, how much love she had lavished on the little room.

'Here she comes.'

We turned expectantly towards the door.

She was wearing face powder, a sure sign that she had been crying. Father drew her chair up to the range and I went to get a cup and saucer from the dresser.

'No tea, thank you.'

'But you must be –'

Her look silenced me.

'I'm sorry, Mother,' I began again.

'I don't wish to discuss it, Ellen. There is nothing to discuss.'

I knew that this was merely the formal introduction to the tirade and I sat back, prepared to listen but determined to remain unmoved. In the silence I could hear her

29

draw in her breath. Then father spoiled the effect by clearing his throat.

'I haven't said anything before, Frances,' – the use of her Christian name was somehow shocking, unnamed as she always was in family conversations – 'but I think you shouldn't take on too badly about all this.'

Mother swatted him aside with a distracted gesture and prepared to marshal the powers of her oratory once more.

'I mean, the way I look at it is – I don't think it would altogether be a bad thing if Ellen moved into a flat with her little friend.'

We both stared at him in disbelief. Father's opinion was neither sought nor offered in family crises and that he should voice such an unorthodox belief now was far beyond my understanding of him.

'I've been thinking. It's . . . it hasn't been easy for Ellen over the years. I mean, she's been too much in our concern . . . there's no distraction in this house, nothing to take our minds off her. Not that I'm blaming you for that, but it can be a bit of a burden for a young girl to carry.'

Mother's mouth had formed itself into a dark O of astonishment.

'You think about it anyway. The change might do us all a lot of good.'

He walked to the dresser and took down his book from behind the plates. Mother sat as if in a catatonic trance, her skimpy beige eyebrows disappearing into her hairline. And for the four weeks that I remained at home, I remembered them like that, raised in an expression of permanent surprise.

There was no more opposition from her. She went into shock, and though her housekeeping was as meticulous as ever, it lacked the aggression of former days and there was much less banging of saucepan lids and sloshing of water on floors. The focus of her attention had shifted also. Her eyes followed father now, though furtively. I could see that he would not be taken for

30

granted again. He had changed too, though in some more subtle manner. His silences now seemed to fill the house, whereas before, not hearing him, I very often didn't see him. He continued to sit in the second best fireside chair and to read his paperbacks – Nat Gould and Edgar Wallace. And his mannerisms no longer irritated me – licking his thumb before turning a page, spelling out the difficult words under his breath. When he settled down to read, I found myself tiptoeing around him.

Now I wanted to be off, to be moving, to be quickly settled in my new home. I itched in the uncertainty of the present. But Myra held back. 'This is an important decision, we mustn't rush into anything.'

'We haven't even started looking.'

'We will tomorrow. We'll buy an early edition of the evening paper and set about the whole thing methodically.'

I hadn't realized how difficult it would prove. For the next three weeks we trudged through the inner suburbs, those semi-derelict tracts of land where family houses had been turned into flats and bed-sitters. We trudged up garden paths and down basement steps. I became an expert on smells: mouse, drains, dry rot. Most of the habitable places we couldn't have afforded, but there were several possibilities which Myra dismissed with hardly a glance round. 'I couldn't live here,' she'd say, sniffing the air like a setter. 'The feeling is all wrong.' Or it was too suburban or the wallpaper was depressing. I was sure she would never be satisfied, not with what we could afford to pay.

'Myra, can't you do it on your own?' I said one night as my nerves finally cracked.

'How can I decide without you? We're both going to live in the place.'

'I don't care – I'll like anything you pick out.'

'That's what's wrong with you, Ellen, you don't even know what you want. Okay, I'll decide. I suppose it'll be quicker that way. Only don't blame me if you're not satisfied.'

*     *     *

31

'It's a nice area,' Myra said, 'Donnybrook is still quite select. And we can both get one bus to work, we don't have to change. You see, Ellen, that's what I kept telling you. I had a lot of angles to consider when I was choosing this flat.'

We were walkling along a road of tall houses. They were built in pairs, with doors and windows set in Gothic arches. The redbrick was raw and clashed with the colours of the stained glass, set in panels on either side of the doors. The effect was one of ecclesiastical gloom, added to by the echoing emptiness of the street. I thought it would be a depressing place to live.

Myra opened the gate of No. 42. The cement path was broken here and there, with weeds growing through the cracks.

'The bell doesn't work.' Myra was banging on the door with her fist.

It was opened by a tall man who stared at us in alarm. He wore a green baize apron, and the sun, catching his glasses, gave him a blind look.

'Don't you remember me, Mr Harvey-Brown? I came yesterday – about the flat.'

'Oh? Oh, yes, now I remember. You know your way then Miss – m'm – nothing is locked.'

We climbed upwards, three flights of stairs, until our ascent was halted by a brown door. Myra flung it open.

'Voilà!'

I stepped back, blinded by the sudden explosion of light. Then, shading my eyes with my hand, I moved forward. I was in a long attic room, running the length of the house, I guessed. The ceiling, quite low, sloped downwards towards three white walls; the fourth wall, the source of the dazzling light, was made entirely of glass. I stepped into a sunbeam and turned my face towards the warmth. Tension slipped from the tips of my fingers and I stretched with pleasure.

'There's no furniture,' I said indifferently.

'She'll supply anything we want, Mrs Harvey-Brown.' Myra slipped a hand through my arm. 'Well? Isn't it utter perfection? Wasn't I right to hold out?'

She had been right, of course she had been right. We walked towards the glass wall and looked out. Down below, impossibly distant, a back garden lay in savage dormancy; on the skyline little hills crouched bluely against the cold. Up here, all was quiet and remoteness. I felt myself afloat on top of the world.

'Let's move in as soon as possible,' I said.

We groped our way downwards towards the kitchen, our eyes adjusting slowly to the comparative dark. Mrs Harvey-Brown sat in a wheelchair with her son behind her. They might have been posing for a Victorian photograph.

'You'll take it of course.' Her voice, unlike her son's, sounded English.

'Yes, but there are a few things –'

'Henry will see to all that, Henry is my factotum.'

Henry nodded.

'It used to be my studio. Did you notice the light? Yes, I painted up there for five years, the happiest years of my life. That's why I was reluctant to let it – other people walking over my dreams. But,' she smiled at Myra, 'I took a liking to you, girl. You know, I could have amounted to something, I had talent and vision. All brought to nothing by this wretched boy.' She drove an elbow into Henry's middle-aged paunch. 'Great lumpen schoolboy. I was rushing downstairs to get his lunch. He couldn't be late for a rugby match or some equally important engagement. I fell and broke my back and I've been in this thing ever since. And I've never been able to paint again, isn't that strange? Useless,' she clapped her hands together, 'utterly useless, just like my back. Now, you can discuss furniture later with Henry.'

Henry nodded again and beamed at us.

'If that's all settled then, I think we should have a drink to celebrate.'

With a spin of the wheel, Mrs. Harvey-Brown propelled herself across the kitchen and, rooting around in a cupboard, produced a bottle of gin.

33

'Gin and water? If you stick to water the gin will never do you any harm. It's those fizzy drinks that play havoc with your insides.'

She half-filled a tumbler and then handed it to Henry who thrust in under the tap. 'Yes, me back was broken and I was stuck in this contraption. Still, I've had the consolation of being looked after by a devoted son.' She cackled up at him. 'Now, who's going to join me? No? Perhaps it is a bit early for young livers.'

Henry saw us to the front door.

'You make out a list for me and I'll have everything you need. Just let me know when you decide to move in, I'd like to have everything spick and span.'

'It will be soon.'

'Good.'

'I'll drop round a list tomorrow evening.'

'Good. Splendid.'

'That man's so vague,' Myra said, as he stood waving at the door. 'I just hope we can depend on him to get everything we need up there.'

Father carried my suitcase to the bus stop on the back of his bike. I thought that mother would at least come to the door but she remained at the kitchen table, polishing her EPNS tea service.

'I'm off then,' I said, forcing myself back into the little room.

She looked up indifferently. 'I'd keep an umbrella handy if I were you,' was all she said. But I had heard her weeping during the night.

The rain had begun before we got to the bus stop. We stood in the downpour and father lifted my suitcase and placed it under the shelter of a garden wall.

'It'll be great to get rid of you, have the house to ourselves for a change,' he said, thrusting two pound notes into my hand. 'I won't wait for the bus. I'll ... well, anyway, you know where we are if you want anything.' And he cycled off, vulnerable as a baby on his high, old-fashioned bike.

I was to meet Myra outside Clery's. If she hadn't caught sight of me I think I might have turned round and got the bus home. She waved, scowling, surrounded by various bits of luggage. 'You're late.'

I was five minutes early.

'Anyway, never mind that, help me get a taxi.'

I felt the two pound notes in my pocket. 'We can get the bus just outside the Savoy.'

'Oh, for heaven's sake. I'll pay, if that's what's worrying you. I've no intention of arriving at the Harvey-Brown's like a country bumpkin.'

Suddenly, it was all too much. I turned away so that Myra would not see my tears. How I wished that I was returning to my thin-walled cell, my refuge for as long as I could remember. The faded paint, the cracks in the ceiling, every tear in its linoleum was familiar and, now, dear. Tomorrow morning I would wake up in that strange glass room and I would listen to the breathing of a stranger, just a few feet away. I drew over to my side of the taxi and looked out the window.

'What's wrong with you, Ellen?' Myra was shaking my averted shoulder. 'Aren't you excited? Think of all the fun we'll have. We'll have at homes and dinner parties and garden parties in the summer – if we can get that fellow to cut the grass. And I'm a very good cook, but you needn't worry, I know all about calories. I'll have you losing weight in no time and you won't even know you're hungry.'

I blushed. How silly of me to imagine that just because she had never mentioned it, Myra hadn't noticed my weight.

The rain fell steadily and the city streets squelched past, unfamiliar and hostile. The taxi driver whistled 'I'll Take You Home Again, Kathleen' through his teeth and Myra lurched against me as we sailed round a corner.

'I can't wait,' she said, seeking my hand. 'I can't wait for our new life to begin.'

\*      \*      \*

35

I snuggled into the blankets. It was so cold in the studio that my face actually ached. The wind rattled the cardboard in the empty grate and raindrops threw themselves in a frenzy against the glass wall. The bed-socks I wore hadn't prevented my feet from turning numb. I slipped out of bed and tiptoed over to the oil heater. When the wick had caught I put on the top and shuffled back to bed. I listened to Myra's breathing. It was barely audible, like a baby's, and I knew that she would sleep like that until I woke her with a cup of tea. It was Sunday, the best day of the week. We would put the chicken in the oven before going to last Mass, and we'd leave the oil heater on low. When we got back, the studio would be warm but we'd still light a fire. After dinner we might read or wash our hair and listen to the radio. We always had tea by the fire, tinned salmon sandwiches perhaps, and a cake. Myra allowed us cake on a Sunday.

We had been in the studio six weeks and I still woke every morning with a sense of wonder. Usually I woke early, wrenched from sleep by the cold. But as I huddled under the bedclothes and realization of where I was began to penetrate my shivering consciousness, my body started to throb with gratitude, pushing back any sensation of cold. My own flat, my own friend, my own life. Actions were meaningful now, days no longer merely to be endured. Sitting in the launderette was a source of pleasure, washing-up a voluptuous task. I could think of no way in which my life could be improved, no desire which was not fulfilled. All I wanted was to be grounded in the here and now, to go on like this, for ever.

Myra stirred and I turned up the gas so that the kettle came back to the boil. As I poured the tea, she sat up, rubbing her eyes. Pretty Myra, all pink cheeks and shining curls; there was never any suggestion of early morning frowstiness about her. She sipped her tea and smiled across at me. I got her dressing-gown from behind the door and placed it round her shoulders, thinking what pleasure I got from anticipating her wishes.

36

'Ellen?'

'M'm?'

'I've been thinking – why don't we throw our first dinner party?'

My heart lurched against my ribs.

'Don't look so stricken, I don't mean anything very grand. I just thought it would be nice to have the Harvey-Browns up. What do you say?'

No, if I had the courage; no, a thousand times no. I couldn't cope with dinner parties, mother's tea parties had been bad enough. And I didn't need them – but Myra apparently did. Well, I had known that, I had known that I could never be all to Myra as she was to me. But I was having to face up to it sooner than I had expected.

'Here, throw me over that magazine, will you. I came across a lovely recipe, that's what made me think of the dinner party. Here it is – *Rognons Oporto*. Kidneys in port wine. Doesn't that sound swanky?'

I had never eaten kidneys, mother was prejudiced against them. She said that no matter how well you washed them or how long you cooked them, they still tasted of you-know-what.

'And if we ask them, they'll have to ask us back. There's method in my madness, Ellen. I'm sure Mrs Harvey-Brown knows lots of interesting people, artists, and – and Protestants. I mean the sort of people we *ought* to be mixing with.'

I sat thinking with horror of our first social undertaking.

'Well – why don't you say something?'

'Sorry.'

'I know what it is, you think I'm a snob.'

'No I don't.'

'You do, I know you do.'

I handed her a pile of clothes from the back of a chair and she began to get dressed under the blankets. It was a method of dressing she was perfecting, the only way, she said, to beat the cold. Her voice reached me through the bedclothes.

37

'I'm really not a snob, but let's face it – who are we ever going to meet if we don't do something about it, you at that workshop and me at the library? Everyone I know is so dull – I want to meet exciting people, romantic people. Listen, Ellen,' – she jumped out of bed, dressed, and came to sit beside me – 'I've something to tell you if you promise you won't laugh. It's something that happened to me a few years ago and I've never forgotten it.'

She had been a schoolgirl, she told me, home from boarding school and out for a Sunday afternoon walk. Bored with the meandering country road, she had crossed over a crumbling estate wall and into the grounds of Knaresborough. She remembered vaguely hearing that it was a house lived in by elderly recluses. As she was forcing her way through the undergrowth, she was stopped by a yell behind her.

'I was terrified, Ellen. This old woman stood there, in a man's raincoat and wellingtons. She was holding a dead rabbit by its hind legs and she waved it at me.

' "What are you doing here, girl? What do you want?"

' "Nothing, I was just exploring."

' "What's yer name?" That's the way she spoke, sort of country mixed up with English. When I told her who I was she asked me if my father was one of the quacks in town. That made me laugh. Then she told me I could stay and make myself useful! Ellen, it was awful. She made me go round with her, dragging rabbits out of traps. We collected about ten and one of them wasn't dead. She just broke its neck with her hands and shoved it into the bag with the others. Then she asked me to stay to dinner. Can you imagine? The last thing I wanted was food, but I was too scared to say no.'

They went up together to the big house and immediately Myra had been captivated. 'It was the way we came upon it. We were just walking along another path through the trees and suddenly we were out on a sweep of gravel and there was the house. At first, I thought it was made of gold, the way the sun was shining on all the windows.'

38

They went into a sort of scullery to wash their hands and then Constance (that was the woman's name, Constance Oliver) had said, 'Come and meet my brother, Willie, he's sure to be in the drawing-room at this time.' Then Constance had left her with Willie, who talked to her about calligraphy and showed her various manuscripts, until Constance called them to the kitchen for dinner.

The dinner was worse, she said, even than she was used to – rabbit, of course, with bits of fur still attached. Afterwards, they returned to the drawing-room for coffee.

'It's a funny thing, Ellen, the way we say something is beautiful. I mean, I might say a dress is beautiful or some film star, but I never thought of a house as beautiful until I saw theirs. That drawing-room – I'd never been in a room like it before. You couldn't say it wasn't shabby and I don't think it was very clean, but it was magical. It was so – sort of open, not like a room at all, with the high ceiling and three windows right down to the ground. And the walls were covered in pink silk. Imagine it, Ellen! I'd never even thought of such a thing before. The carpet told a story, Willie explained it to me. I was afraid to walk on it, it was almost threadbare. It was Chinese, creamy-white with pink figures.'

Myra paused for a while, turning away a dreaming face.

'I think that's why it affected me so much, because it was all so fragile. It seemed to me that if I blew really hard the whole thing would collapse. But there it was, shimmering in the evening light. Beauty is like that, isn't it, Ellen? If you grasp at it, it disappears.

'Anyway, Constance asked me to come and visit them again but she was dead before I went back to school. I heard Daddy talking about it one night. She got a haemorrhage to the brain and she was dead before he got there. Willie had cycled in for him, cursing the fact that he had never learned to drive, but Daddy said it would have been too late anyway.

'Then Willie went off somewhere and the house was shut up. I've never been back but I heard that it's just a ruin now. Tinkers break in from time to time and then the guards go along and board up another window. Nobody really cares though; most people think that it's a good thing that the Olivers have gone at last.'

We sat in silence for a while and I imagined the house as it had been. I was affected by Myra's story, with its echoes of my own, my Sligo romance.

'Do you understand, Ellen? When Constance died and Willie disappeared I felt a real sense of loss, even though I'd only just met them. If it wasn't such a silly thing to say, I'd say I'd fallen in love with them, or with their world anyway. And when I came to Dublin, I said to myself that I was going to find it again, I was determined to do that. So you see . . . Mrs Harvey-Brown is a bit like that, romantic I mean. And I thought . . .'

She let her sentence trail off and was looking embarrassed again.

How perfectly I understood her emotions. And I could afford to be generous. Here I was, living out my romance, surely I could help Myra to rekindle hers?

'I think a dinner party is a very good idea. And I'll buy the wine. And I think the Rognons Oporto sound marvellous, I'm sure that's the sort of thing Mrs Harvey-Brown is used to eating, not chicken or something dull like that. It'll be the best dinner party ever, Myra, just you wait and see.'

'Ellen! What am I going to do?'

We were both standing, staring at the glutinous mess in the saucepan. The kidneys stared back, glistening maliciously in their lumpish, purple sauce. Rognons Oporto had been bubbling steadily for forty minutes but when pierced with a fork – no easy task – they gushed blood.

'Put them back for another ten minutes or so.'

'I can't, the sauce is too thick already.'

'Add some water.'

40

'Don't be stupid, Ellen Yates – water would ruin the flavour.'

I wondered if at this stage it mattered.

'I've got it!'

Grabbing a bottle of Australian burgundy she began to pour it in a steady stream into the saucepan. I had opened two bottles at four o'clock on Myra's instructions. I had been impressed when she had explained how they needed to breathe. Now the well-aired wine was turning the sauce from purple into mauvey-pink.

'You and I will just have to go easy on the wine. Will half a glass do you? And you can have two sherries beforehand.'

The studio looked lovely. Myra had spent ages trying to achieve what she called a Bohemian effect. She said that Mrs Harvey-Brown, having been an artist, would appreciate that. She had hidden the cooker and sink behind a bedspread pinned with drawing-pins to the ceiling and then had sellotaped postcards here and there on the bedspread to disguise its real nature. She had bought five Christmas candles, which, pared down, fitted into the necks of wine bottles and these were strategically placed around the room. When we heard the Harvey-Browns on the stairs, I was to start lighting them and she would turn off the electricity. She had even bought cushion covers for our pillows which were now strewn around the two beds. They were, as a result, supposed to look like sofas; I thought they still looked like beds. Nevertheless, I had to admit the studio was transformed.

'They're coming.'

For a moment we were too panic-stricken to move. Then I began to light the candles and Myra went to the door to welcome them in.

When I saw them, I was glad that we had gone to so much trouble, for evidently so had they. Mrs Harvey-Brown, in Henry's arms, wore a long black dress. Henry had on a velvet jacket and spotted bow tie. I thought he very nearly looked handsome.

'Well, girls, let's get the party going.' Mrs Harvey-Brown produced a bottle of gin as Henry lowered her into our best chair. 'Just a small sherry for this child of mine. He's my navigator and I don't want to end up falling down those stairs again.'

I poured sherry for Henry and myself, the other two had gin. Myra had warned me beforehand that I must make an effort to keep the conversation going, that I must pull my weight if there were pauses. She needn't have worried – there weren't any. Mrs Harvey-Brown saw to that.

'Call me Edith,' she had said at the beginning, as Myra and I brought extra cushions to prop her up.

'You really are dear girls. I was worried at first that you might be the quiet sort, you know, off to bed at eight o'clock with cocoa and the Rosary, Henry here is a bit that way inclined, not the Rosary, obviously, but he does favour cocoa and virtue. Takes after my husband I'm afraid, a very boring man. Do you know, we were married for twenty-one years and for all those years he ate exactly the same breakfast – a three-minute egg, two slices of brown bread and marge and two cups of tea without sugar.' She paused to refill her glass. 'Can you begin to imagine it, girls? Every single morning, the same thing. Made no difference what day it was – Christmas, Ramadan, my birthday, always the same. And he did yoga. Used to sit in front of an open window in a loin cloth running bits of strings through his nostrils. Disgusting.' She shuddered at the memory.

'Of course he was very vain. I never knew until after we were married that he wore a corset. He *was*, handsome, I'll give him that – that's why I married him. But it is foolish to fall for a pretty face – let you girls be warned. Henry.'

'Yes, Mother?'

'Stand up.'

Henry did as he was told.

'No great beauty there, you can see that. But I can assure you that Henry would make an excellent husband. He is kind and biddable and, really, no woman can ask for more in a spouse.'

Henry beamed and stuck out his chin.

'Dinner,' Myra shouted, banging our tin tray with a spoon. The evening and Myra were becoming less refined and I felt we were all going to enjoy ourselves.

Myra splashed soup onto our plates and then disappeared behind the bedspread where I could hear her muttering and groaning to herself. The soup, tinned consommé to which Myra had added half a bottle of sherry, tasted rather good. The Harvey-Browns had second helpings, which was just as well, as it turned out.

'Ellen,' Myra called.

I held back the bedspread and she made her entrance, bearing a steaming serving dish. From the plate *Rognons Oporto* rose, like Himalayan peaks, and like those mountain peaks the very tops were covered in white. I looked more closely and saw that they were coated in shredded coconut. Around the foothills, covering the glistening purple, were three or four rows of peas and further down the slope there was an orchard of sliced peaches. We stared, stunned into silence.

'Too pretty to eat,' Mrs Harvey-Brown murmured faintly, but Myra was already savaging it with a fork and spoon.

It was certainly too slippery to eat with any comfort. I tried to spear bits of the kidney as they skidded round the plate. The sauce had an unplesant tinny taste, like cheap cutlery, and when I finally managed to capture a piece of kidney, I had to swallow it whole, for chewing seemed to have no effect on its rubbery density.

'Unusual flavour.' Mrs Harvey-Brown took a swig of gin, ignoring the Australian burgundy at her elbow.

Henry seemed to be concentrating on the peas, eating them one at a time, chewing each one with great thoroughness.

Then, without warning, Myra began to slide sideways

43

until she was lying across Henry's knee. 'Myra,' I called out and shook her, but she was fast asleep.

'That's it then.' I could see relief spreading over Mrs Harvey-Brown's face. 'You and Henry carry her over to the bed. There's no point in trying to waken her until she's slept off the gin!'

As she spoke, she was gathering her bag and screwing the top back on the gin bottle.

'But you'll stay and finish your meal?'

'Of course not – that child needs quiet. Besides,' she waved towards the plates of food, 'we were more or less finished. So delicious but rather rich.'

I had set the studio to rights by the time Myra came to. She sat up, then fell back again, holding her head.

'Would you like a cup of tea?' I asked, sitting down beside her. As I watched, her expression changed from incomprehension to horror.

'What time is it?'

'Half-nine.'

'Then – where are the Harvey-Browns?'

'They left ages ago, Mrs Harvey-Brown thought you needed quiet. How do you feel?'

'How could you, Ellen? How could you let them go?'

'I didn't have a chance –'

'They could hardly have started their dinner.' She turned her face to the wall. 'It was a disaster, everything went wrong.'

'Oh Myra, don't worry about it, nobody minded, honestly. It was all just a bit of fun.'

'Oh yes,' she sat up. 'I suppose you all had a giggle at my expense. Fine friend you've turned out to be.'

'Nobody was laughing at you, none of us would do that.'

'Not half. I've really had my eyes opened tonight. Do you know what you are, Ellen? You're a snake in the grass. You make sure you stay sober so that you can be all superior afterwards, but you wouldn't think of advising me. You must have seen that I was drinking too much. Why didn't you stop me?'

44

I was amazed at her anger – nothing awful had happened, after all. And why she should attack me I didn't know either, but it was so unfair that I didn't attempt to defend myself.

'Go on, off with you, I'm fed up of the sight of you. Why don't you go downstairs to your fine friends and have another laugh at my expense.'

In the bathroom I brushed my teeth three times and still the taste of *Rognons Oporto* clung. I spat into the basin and admired the way I was controlling my emotions. Myra's attack had hurt, the hurt had quickly turned to anger but now the anger had dissipated and I was feeling cold and hard and grown-up. I would continue to live in the flat but I would go my own way. And I would not forgive her. At this moment I hated her and thought that it was I who was the fool ever to have seen Myra as anything other than spoilt and selfish. I might even get a bed-sitter and move out after a while. Plenty of people lived on their own and didn't die of loneliness.

The door handle rattled.

'Let me in for God's sake.'

Myra fell into the room and over to the lavatory. She knelt in front of the pan, moaning. Even in the weak light from the overhead bulb I could see that her face was green.

'I think I'm going to die, Ellen.'

I held her head and shushed her.

'Why did I drink that gin – why did I do it? I don't even like gin.'

I flushed the lavatory and she bent over it again.

'I'm so stupid, such a fool. I wish I was like you, Ellen, grown-up and mature. I'm just a fool, a fool.'

I washed her face and supported her up the stairs. In bed, she was asleep before I had finished tucking her in. The little face looked as sweet as ever under its wreath of curls. I left the plastic basin beside her bed and turned out the light.

\*　　\*　　\*

45

We had been in the flat six months and in that time I had become a reader. Myra had persuaded me to join the library and on her late night I went there from work, changed my books, and waited for her until closing time. It was nice making the journey home together.

I read mainly light romances, not in any sense of expectation but more as others read science fiction. There was a favourite theme, however, in these books, which I adopted and applied to my own little world – that of the straying husband. The theme developed with the synchronous truth that the wife always sensed intuitively what was going on before she was told anything. Although I could hardly apply straying to any of Myra's actions in relation to me, I, too, trembled with an intuitive and unwelcome knowledge: Myra was in love.

There had been boyfriends before, but this was different. I watched her covertly as she prepared for dates, and saw a change, not so much in her behaviour as in her essence. There was a new and strange lack of definition about her, a continual breaking up and re-forming of her personality as if she suddenly didn't know who she was. There was a sighing over eyebrows too, but that was more to be expected.

When Myra and I had moved in, Myra had said sternly, 'There will be no boyfriends, Ellen. It just gets your name up if you have men dropping in when they feel like it. When we invite a man back here, it will be somebody important.'

So I waited now.

It came one Saturday night as I stood scraping scrambled egg off a saucepan.

'Ellen.'

'Yes?'

'Are you in tonight?'

Was I ever anything else?

'It's just – you know what we said about inviting people in and all that. Well – there's somebody I'd like to ask back tonight, someone I'd like you to meet.'

I forced a smile and asked who.

46

'Oh Ellen, I've been dying to tell you about it but I'm so nervous, I've been terrified to say a word about it in case it all went poof.'

'Who is he?'

'He's wonderful, he's quite different from any other boy I've been out with. I knew the minute I saw him that this was it. They say you can always tell the real thing. You'll love him, Ellen.'

Silly Myra.

'He's taking me to the pictures this evening and I thought I'd ask him in for a coffee afterwards, if that's all right with you. I mean, would it suit you? I don't want to upset your plans.'

She must really be feeling nervous, I thought sourly, to show such regard for my convenience.

'I'll have the coffee ready when you come back.'


Adrien West overflowed from our best armchair and looked around him with an air of complacency. He was dressed in a tweed suit and had broad pink hands and a wide schoolboy face. He looked very clean, shining and well-scrubbed, and I thought of the years he must have stood in line while school matrons checked behind his ears. He was a grown-up Christopher Robin, a type, a visual cliché, and Myra had fallen for something familiar and sought after but out of reach.

'It's not exactly cosy, is it?' he said, pointing to the glass wall. 'Don't you feel a bit exposed, without curtains or blinds or something?'

'There's nobody to see us but the stars,' Myra replied with awful coyness.

'And the man in the moon.' He included me in his laugh.

He was like that, easy and unselfconscious so that everything he said sounded either witty or intelligent. He sat back, crossing his legs neatly at the ankle, like a well brought up girl. Despite his size there was something girlish about him, in his mannerisms, the way he turned his head. A mammy's boy.

Myra sat on the edge of her chair, listening to him respectfully. I was irritated by her awe of him. I was overwhelmed myself but then that was perfectly natural – the only men I had ever spoken to up till now were Henry, Jack Taylor and my father. So I had every reason to blush and fumble, but not Myra. She looked so pretty tonight with her cheeks flushed and her features quicksilver with shyness, and yet I could see that he was taking all this loveliness for granted. I felt like banging both their heads together so that they might see what I saw.

'Well – what do you think?' She hadn't spoken until the sound of his car engine faded.

'He seems a nice enough chap,' I said cautiously, trying to meet her half-way.

'Nice! Don't be so dull – he's wonderful. Isn't he very polished, Ellen, you must have noticed that. He went to Trinity and he's got a degree in Economics. Guess what he does?'

'I couldn't.'

'He's a stockbroker.'

Now that really did impress me. In the novels I read the husbands were often stockbrokers, but I hadn't realized until now that we had any in Ireland.

'And he plays cricket in the summer. I mean, Ellen, he's the real thing.'

I could see that. 'Is he from Dublin?'

'Nearly, he's from Greystones. He lives with his mother, his father is dead and he has only one sister, in Rhodesia I think. She's called Robin. Isn't that a queer name for a girl? What's it like, Greystones?'

I'd been there only once, a quiet seaside village with an ugly beach. 'It's very quiet, not the sort of place you'd go for the day. I remember my father used to say it was the most Protestant village in Ireland.'

'It sounds wonderful. Oh, I hope he invites me there soon, even though I'd be frightened to death of meeting his mother. He's taking me beagling on Sunday. I wonder

48

what I should wear? It wouldn't do to turn up in the wrong thing. I'm really excited. Ellen – I know I won't sleep a wink tonight.'

But it was I who remained awake as the hours passed. I threshed and tossed and finally, giving up the struggle, went to sit by the glass wall, wrapped in a blanket. There were no stars in the sky, just gaping black. Gradually however, as my eyes adjusted, I could decipher the denser outlines of varying shapes. Things crouched against the tarry night, distinct and separate in their isolation. If there was a God out there, he was well and truly asleep.

Staring into the night, I admitted to myself my worry. This would be no casual affair, not as far as Myra was concerned. I wondered how long she had been seeing him. Obviously long enough to see herself as going steady. And going steady leads to engagement and engagement to . . .

I *could* live on here by myself, it wouldn't be that bad. I'd have my library books and my radio. I could call on the Harvey-Browns and maybe Myra would come to visit.

The formality of the phrase catapulted me into the future. I saw a matronly Myra walking up the front path, children in tow. I had always known that this would happen some day, that Myra was not going to spend her life in the studio with me. But that was for the future, not now. Now was the time for us, for girlhood. Life would carry us along with its own gross energy but I wanted now for me.

I got back into bed and began to suck my frozen fingers. The throb of returning life eased the other, more pervasive pain and I tried to concentrate on the pulsing tips. Had mother felt like this as she lay in the darkness the night before I left home? I remembered the muffled sobbing coming through the thin wall and how it had irritated me.

But how senseless, this child's game of tig – mother pursued me and I pursued Myra and now Myra reached

49

out for Adrien. I laughed into the blanket and, consoled by the sheer absurdity of it all, sleep came at last.

Myra drew the paraffin heater nearer to the dressing table and peered at her face in the glass. I lay on the bed and watched her, as I often did when she was getting ready for a date. She usually saw Adrien twice a week although she only brought him in occasionally. She told me that he found the studio made him light-headed, with all that glass.

She sighed now as she scrubbed out her mouth and painted in a new one.

'I can't get the colour right. This pink dress is impossible to match.' She scowled at her reflection in the mirror. 'Ellen – tell me the truth. Do I look tarty?'

I laughed. Could a cherub look tarty? 'You look lovely.'

She turned to stare at her reflection again but seemed to find nothing there to reassure her. 'I'm fed up to the teeth.'

'What's wrong?'

She came and sat beside me on the bed and her little face crumpled like an unironed handkerchief.

'I sometimes wonder if it's worth all the effort.'

I felt a stab of hope. 'Are you getting fed up with Adrien?'

'How could you ask such a question?'

'Then what's wrong with you? You're seeing enough of him and I don't think he's even been late for one date in the past three months.'

Moodily, she sat staring at her lipstick, swivelling it up and down. She threw it towards the dressing table and it landed on the floor. I bent to retrieve it.

'It's not progressing.'

'What's not?'

'Our relationship.'

I thought about that one. 'Do you mean that he hasn't asked you to marry him?'

'Now that's a really stupid thing to say. Do you think that all I'm interested in is hooking a husband? I thought you'd have known me better than that by now. Anyway,' she shook her curls, 'I consider myself far too young for marriage.'

I let out my breath.

'It's just that – I don't know, I never seem to get anywhere near him. I mean, he never really has a conversation with me, just jokes and that, and you know, Ellen, we're never on our own, we always have to meet crowds of his friends, he never seems to *want* to be on his own with me.'

'At least he's not ashamed of you.'

'No, because I'm fairly presentable I suppose, but that's all. I feel I'm nothing special to him, I could be one of a dozen girls. I'm not special the way he is to me.'

'I'm sure that's not true.' I could afford to give reassurance now. 'I'm sure he wouldn't take you out if he felt like that. I mean, it's not as if there was any shortage of girls in Dublin.'

'Oh, I don't know.'

'Could you try playing hard to get?' I suggested, applying what so often worked in the novels I read.

'I couldn't, I'd be afraid to take the risk. I do love him, Ellen, I really do.'

When she had gone, I made myself a cup of tea and twiddled the knob on the radio until I found some music. I took my tea over to the glass wall and sat looking down. Things were beginning to grow, there was noticeably more green around than there had been a week ago.

I couldn't take Myra's worry seriously. Adrien was far too self-satisfied ever to fall in love, at least in the way Myra meant. But he obviously liked her and *she* might well be the one who eventually got fed up. In the meantime, I was sure that he would continue to take her out.

I turned up the radio and danced my way over to the sink. That was one of the advantages of the studio – we were so far up there was no danger of disturbing the Harvey-Browns.

\* \* \*

51

She woke me that night when she came home. She sat on my bed and tickled my face. 'Ellen,' she whispered, 'Ellen, I've something I want to tell you.'

I pulled the light cord and looked up at her shining face. My God! Had I been wrong then? Had he –?

'I'm going to the theatre next week, Ellen, at last I've got him to take me somewhere on my own.'

I relaxed back onto my pillows. 'That's great.'

'He's taking me to the Abbey – what do you think of that! I took your advice, even though my heart was in my mouth. I was very cool all evening and when he said, casual as usual, that he'd see me on Saturday, I said I didn't know, that I was pretty fed up of pubs.'

'Good for you.'

'Then he just asked me what I'd like to do and I said go to the theatre. I don't even know what the play is and I don't care. He said he'll get the tickets tomorrow just to be sure. And I'd never have done it without you.'

She gave me a hug and went off, singing, to the bathroom.

I pulled the blankets over my ears and kicked the hot water bottle, now quite cold, onto the floor. Tomorrow was my library day and we planned to buy fish and chips on our way home for our tea. Friday night was our night for cleaning the studio. On Saturday, when Myra had gone to the theatre, Henry would probably ask me down for a cup of tea. He often did that when Myra went out on a date and I knew he did it out of kindness because he felt sorry for me. I stretched my body and thought of the sheer voluptuousness of my life – fish and chip suppers, tea by the fire, secrets shared with a friend. There was no detail of my life that I would change; Henry's pity was quite misplaced.

'I'll phone the library and tell them you won't be in.'

From the bed, Myra gave me a miserable little smile. Her cold was at its streaming worst, the first one she'd had since we moved into the studio.

'Don't worry,' I reassured her, 'I'm sure you'll be much better by tonight.'

'I don't care how I feel – I'll get to that theatre if it kills me. How do I look though, how will I look tonight with my swollen nose and pink eyes?'

'Well, the fire's lit and the lemonade is on the table. I'll be back by two and we'll see how things are then. No point in worrying now.'

She was asleep when I got back though the fire was still aglow and the studio quite warm. I tucked the blankets round her and sat by the fire to wait.

'I'm hungry,' was the first thing she said. 'I must be a lot better, Ellen, this is the first time I've felt like eating since Thursday.'

I warmed some soup for us and brought her a bowl.

'The colour was an inspired choice, wasn't it?' She waved her spoon towards a red dress hanging on the wardrobe door. 'I was dithering between the blue and the red and the shop girl was trying to make me take the blue, but the red is definitely more cheerful and that's what I need tonight. Here, give it over to me, and the little mirror.'

I held the mirror and she raised the red material to her face. Then, sitting up, she grabbed the glass and started examining her chin.

'Oh no! Ellen – why didn't you tell me?'

I looked more closely at her face. 'Is it that little cold sore?'

'Little? You must be blind – it's the size of an onion. That's it then – I can't go.'

'Of course you can.'

'Looking like this? Red eyes and cold sores and swollen nose! Indeed I can't. Anyway, they probably wouldn't let me in. They would probably think I was in the early stages of leprosy.'

I laughed. 'Stop exaggerating, Myra. Just put on some face powder and nobody will even notice.'

'You think Adrien wouldn't notice? That's all you know. He hates make-up and if I start covering myself in powder it will only draw his attention to my disfigurement.'

53

I thought she was better off in bed in any case, she looked very flushed. 'You probably wouldn't enjoy it anyway, Myra, your cold is still very heavy. Give me Adrien's phone number and I'll go and phone him.'

Myra lay back, moaning. 'Isn't it just my luck, it's just the sort of thing that happens to me. You'll have to go then, Ellen, instead of me. Make me another bowl of soup and then you'd better be getting ready.'

I was aghast. 'But I don't have to go; can't I ring and tell him?'

'No – I'm not letting Adrien out on his own on a Saturday night in Dublin. You'll *have* to go.'

'I couldn't. I'd do anything for you but I couldn't go to the theatre with Adrien.'

'Don't be so selfish, kicking up such a fuss about a little thing like that.'

'Anyway I've nothing to wear to a theatre.'

'For heaven's sake, what does that matter? Nobody is going to notice you. Adrien isn't going to be interested one way or the other in how you look. Just put on a coat and go.'

A churning sensation had begun in my stomach and my body blushed at the thought of the embarrassment of spending an evening in the company of Adrien. And yet I suppose Myra was right – he would hardly notice me.

'Please, Ellen, just for me. I know that fellow. He wouldn't waste those tickets, he'd ask someone else. Please, please, please. I know he'd be safe with you.'

I arrived far too early at the theatre. In the brightly lit foyer I felt the ushers looking at me with curiosity. With relief, my eyes caught sight of a door marked Ladies, and I slunk inside. I washed my hands, combed my hair, then washed my hands again. It was warm in there and I undid my coat buttons. My old navy jersey stared at me from the full-length mirror, shabbier than ever under the neon strip light; further down my hips spread and my ankles bulged. I was almost surprised by my appearance, for since moving in with Myra I had stopped thinking of myself as ugly. Maybe I had assumed, unconsciously, that living within the perimeter of such beauty I, too, would be transformed.

I smiled jeeringly at my old, familiar face and Myra's words of the afternoon came back to me: 'What does it matter what you wear, he'll be safe with you.'

Suddenly I was angry with her – not for seeing me as I was, but for being so careless of my feelings that she could tell me what she saw. An ugly woman was no less a woman, and my anger now was urging me to make a declaration of my womanhood, even if it also made me look foolish.

I scrabbled around in my bag and rooted out a lipstick and a little pot of foundation. I had bought them on impulse more than a year ago and they had remained, unused, in my bag ever since. Now I spread the brown, creamy liquid over my face and watched my pimples disappear. I filled in my mouth in Walnut Bronze and shook the hairpins from my hair.

I looked at my reflection and I felt a sudden heat between my legs. I wasn't at all sure that I looked any better, but, in putting on make-up, I was making a statement, and I was excited by the statement. For no reason I felt a surge of confidence, as if I were unbruisable behind my mask. The alchemous power of Outdoor Girl would see me through the evening.

I ran to meet Adrien and touched him on the sleeve. At first he didn't seem to recognize me.

'It's me.'

'Oh? Ellen.'

I explained about Myra.

'Poor old thing and she really wanted to see this play. Do you, or would you prefer if we did something else?'

Before I could answer, he had decided for us. 'No, come on, we might as well go in and see it. It'll pass the time anyway.'

I had never been out with a man before and I had never been inside a theatre in my life, and yet my nonchalance wasn't assumed as I followed the usher to my seat. My anxiety, floating away, had left me light-headed, slightly drunk. As we sat down, our thighs brushed and I shivered. Confidence surged inside me. I turned to put him at his ease. 'I suppose Greystones is very –'

But he was on his feet and stumbling over mine. 'Will you excuse me, Ellen? I've just seen a couple I know down there and I'd like to have a word with them before the show starts.'

I watched as he chatted to some people in the third row. The woman selling programmes had to tell him that the curtain was about to go up. I decided I'd have to try later, at the interval. There would be more time then, anyway.

During Act One I prepared the remarks I would make at the interval. As the lights went up, I offered one. Adrien looked at me, then yawned. I began again but he had turned his head away, looking round him at the emptying seats.

'Would you like an ice-cream? Stay here and I'll go and get you one.'

By the time he came back, smelling of alcohol, the curtain had gone up on Act Two.

'Sorry,' he said, shoving the ice-cream at me. 'I got caught back there.'

My disappointment changed to indignation. So I could be fobbed off, like a child, with an ice-cream, not good enough to be taken to the bar for a drink. Savagely I licked at the wretched cone and wished I had the courage to stick it into his face. I slurped, and sensed disapproval in his tightening body. I slurped with greater determination.

But by the time I got home I was neither angry nor disappointed. I sat in the bathroom, in my overcoat, scrubbing my face and wondering what had come over me. I understood neither my own behaviour nor the emotions which had prompted it. I wasn't interested in Adrien – I wasn't even interested in men in general. And he was Myra's property. Then what had I expected when our thighs brushed in the darkened theatre and why had I been so stricken when he had failed to return promptly with the ice-cream?

I felt again the extraordinary sense of potency coursing through my body as I marched down the aisle behind the usher, a conqueror amidst the plush and fading gilt. Was that what being a normal woman felt like? Was that how Myra felt every morning when she sat before the mirror, putting on her make-up? I must ask her.

She was sitting up in bed, reading.

'Well?'

'I had a wonderful time.'

She looked at me doubtfully.

'You did?'

'Wonderful.' I set about making the cocoa. 'Myra.'

'Well?'

'What does it feel like to be a woman? I mean –'

'Are you drunk, Ellen Yates? What on earth has got into you? You haven't told me a thing, you haven't even mentioned Adrien. Did he miss me, at least?'

I laughed. 'He was bereft. *I* had a good time but *he* was bored. He said he'll ring you during the week and that he hopes you'll be better soon.'

She smiled at me. 'Wasn't I right to make you go? I knew you'd have a good time. Now, hurry up with that cocoa, will you? I want to get back to sleep.'

Good old Myra; the familiar egotism was reassuring somehow.

I brought the cocoa and we sat and discussed ways and means of getting rid of cold sores.

After Easter, the weather started to improve. Recklessly we began to peel off draught excluder from doors and windows and to open panels in the glass wall. Walking through the Dublin streets, the objective world became a reality; no longer a reflection of, or affront to, my moods, it became a storehouse of pleasure and surprise. The commonplace miracle of spring bludgeoned my senses and sent me reeling back to the studio and Myra whose smile lengthened with the lengthening days.

'Don't you love summer?' She was looking out on Mrs Harvey-Brown's savage garden. 'Soon I'll get brown and I'll be able to leave off these horrible nylons. I'm going to get Adrien to take me to the sea and we can swim and have picnics.'

Her arms were already washed a faint gold and tiny freckles had appeared on her cheekbones.

As we watched, Henry came into view, wheeling his mother in her chair. He disappeared for a moment and returned with a stool and a book. Mrs Harvey-Brown turned her face up to the sun and Henry opened the book. Perhaps he was reading to her.

As we gazed down, Mrs Harvey-Brown suddenly turned her head in our direction. She waved and signalled to us to open the window.

'We're planning a party.'

'What?'

'A cocktail party,' she screamed. 'Henry and I are planning a cocktail party.'

Henry smiled up at us and nodded his head vigorously.

'It must be spring,' Myra murmured.

'Come and discuss it with me tomorrow. You can give me advice on what young people drink nowadays.'

We were about to close the panel when there was another shout. 'You must help me out with the young men too, just in case I'm a bit short. Bring your own and any spare ones you can find. I like to have lots of young men around at a party, it makes things nice and jolly.'

'I'll get Adrien to root someone out for you, Ellen,' said Myra, bounding over to the wardrobe. 'Now, what does one wear to a cocktail party? Let's see what I've got.'

'I'd rather you didn't.'

'Didn't what?'

'Didn't ask Adrien to find someone for me.'

'Well you can't expect me to look after you all evening and if there's a shortage of men you're hardly going to get a look-in.'

As usual, it was the casualness of Myra's brutality which made it hurtful.

'I don't expect you to look after me. I really would prefer if you didn't say anything to Adrien, please Myra.'

She shook her head. 'You are a funny girl sometimes. Anyway, I'll have to get that extra man for Mrs H.B., but if that's the way you want it, you needn't think of him for you. I suppose you can always help Henry with the drinks if you're at a loose end.'

We began to look through Myra's dresses to find something for her to wear. We spread out dresses on one bed and skirts and blouses on the other. Myra rejected them all with a wave of her hand. 'No, I'll just have to get something new – a proper cocktail dress. I'll tell you what.' She turned to me, smiling. 'Let's get you a new dress too, Ellen – why don't we? It will be fun, both of us dressing up together. I think you should wear black, it is slimming, and if I wear pink, it would be a great contrast. Come on, let's have a go at seeing what we can do with you.'

The party was to be held in the drawing-room, where we had never been before. It was underneath our studio, on the first floor, and the Harvey-Browns hadn't used it for years. We had been summoned to arrive half an hour before the rest of the guests, to get things going or lend a hand, whichever might be more appropriate.

'Come in, stop hovering.' Mrs Harvey-Brown was sitting on a sofa, propped up with cushions. 'Sit down. What do you think of the smell?'

We sniffed.

'Joss sticks. This room smelled of overexcited cats so Henry suggested joss sticks. He's a wonderful boy really – so resourceful.' She looked around her and shuddered. 'How I loathe this room. It reminds me of when I first got married. We moved into this house with my mother-in-law because we couldn't afford a place of our own. She was a *ghastly* woman. She terrorized me

59

into holding tea parties in here, every Sunday afternoon. The young bride had to be on display to the family and friends. Can you imagine it – Darjeeling or Earl Grey, lemon or milk? Is it any wonder I turned to gin?'

Henry came in, carrying a tin tray piled high with roughly cut sandwiches.

'Ah, good, the canapés.' Mrs Harvey-Brown beamed at him. 'Now, I want you two darlings to take these round for me. Henry will be busy with the drinks and I want all the old pussies to realize that you two are *friends*, not some sort of paying guests. Lots of them will only come to see how hard up we are. Come then, let's get this party started. What's everyone drinking?'

I had finished a glass of sherry by the time the guests started to arrive. At first they trickled in and then they began to increase until the drawing-room was overflowing. I wondered how she knew so many people.

'Look at the old flames,' Myra nudged me.

A circle of elderly gallants had gathered round Mrs Harvey-Brown's sofa. The wives formed a semi-circle behind, ignored and smiling meekly.

The young people clustered round the table where the drinks were. They called Mrs Harvey-Brown Aunt Edith and slapped Henry on the back in a sort of embarrassed mateyness. They seemed to shout rather than speak.

Myra watched them wistfully. 'Didn't I tell you, Ellen? I knew she'd have the right sort of friends. Aren't they really elegant though?'

'They're noisy.'

'Don't be such a drip, Ellen. It's very bourgeois to be worried about keeping your voice down.'

Nobody paid any attention to us. We stood in the corner with the sandwiches in front of us.

'Here goes,' said Myra, lifting the tray. 'I'm not hanging around until Adrien arrives to rescue me.' And with that she headed for a group at the table.

Henry brought me another glass of sherry. 'I'd introduce you to some of those young people but I don't know their names. They're mostly the children of cousins.'

He stood beside me and we watched the surge and retreat. The only still point in the room was the circle around Mrs Harvey-Brown's sofa where the gallants remained constant in their attention. Some of the wives had begun to droop.

'I do like parties.' Henry sounded like a little boy. 'I like looking on, you know, at all the excitement. I don't even mind the noise, I suppose because I get so little of it. Look.' He pointed towards the door. 'Isn't that Myra's friend?'

Adrien was making his way towards us. I introduced Henry, who twinkled coyly behind his glasses. 'I've seen you going in and out.'

'It was very nice of your mother to invite us. I've brought my cousin along – Bobbie.' He turned to introduce the man standing just behind him, who inclined his head in acknowledgement, and I found myself looking down on a pink, almost hairless scalp.

'Hi!' Myra floated towards us. 'I'm glad you could come, Bobbie. Ellen, can you look after them – ah good, Henry is getting the drinks. See you later then, I'm up to my eyes.'

We turned and watched as she approached one of the noisier groups which opened to admit her and then closed round her. I could hear her laugh over the braying of the others.

Adrien laughed too. 'Myra doing her hostess act. If you'll excuse me, I'm going after one of those sandwiches. I'm starving.'

So I was left with Bobbie. Surreptitiously I glanced across at him. His eyes had the aspic glaze of panic and I feared for the sherry glass in his white-knuckled fist.

I found myself relaxing. 'Shall we sit over there in the window seat? I hate standing around at these things.' I sounded as if I went to cocktail parties every night of the week.

He seated himself as far away from me as possible, thrusting his spine into the wall. As I moved slightly nearer to him, he looked longingly towards the door and even seemed to consider the window behind him. Then he drew out a packet of cigarettes. 'Smoke?' But he had pulled the packet out too far and the contents went fanning onto the floor. As we bent to retrieve them, our heads bumped. I began to laugh but saw from his face, only inches from mine, that he was on the verge of tears.

'Here,' I grabbed his glass. 'You pick them up and I'll get us another drink. I don't smoke anyway.'

I brought him back his sherry and he gulped it like a desert wanderer. For the first time he smiled, uncertainly, but a smile nevertheless.

'Are you from the North?'

He nodded.

'Are you down here on holidays?'

'No, doing a course. Staying with Aunt Violet.'

I guessed that this must be Adrien's mother.

'I like it down here, it's very nice so it is. And Adrien's very good to me. I'm lucky to have family here.' He said all this in a rush and I smiled encouragement.

'Are you – I suppose you're well used to these sort of dos.' His eyes met mine and then shied away.

'They can become boring after a while,' I replied casually.

He raised his eyes again and I recognized the admiration in them.

My situation was novel. Never in my life had my presence caused unease in another. Despite my bulk, most people whom I had brushed up against hardly seemed to notice me. Even as a Sixth Year at school, the First Years had been unimpressed by my presence. And as for men . . .

Yet here was a man hanging on my words, listening with attention to my small talk, nodding with respect at my banalities. Admittedly he was smaller than I, and balding, but he *was* male and he was Adrien's cousin.

'You must get Adrien to bring you round to us for a meal,' I heard myself saying. 'We often have people in – nothing formal, just little supper parties.' I sounded just like Myra.

Bobbie's cheeks turned a deeper pink. 'I'd like that. That would be great, so it would.'

As I was trying to think of some details which would flesh out my exotic life, Adrien arrived back. 'Quite a crush,' he said, sitting down between the two of us. 'Well. And how have you two been getting along?'

All my bashfulness returned and as I gazed into my sherry glass I wished Adrien would take himself off so that I might resume my tête-à-tête. I had been enjoying myself.

'Myra seems to be having a gay old time. I think she fancies herself as a cocktail waitress.'

Neither Bobbie nor I said anything.

'Your landlady is quite a character, isn't she? She's asked me round for a drink on my own next week. She said she thought I had possibilities.'

'She likes company.'

'Yes, well, I've had about enough of this lot. These sort of parties give me a headache, there are so many twittering females around. Are you ready, Bobbie, then? Shall we head off?'

Bobbie gulped what was left of his sherry and stood up. 'It's been a really good party, you'd never get anything like this at home. And – thank you.' He grasped my hand and shook it up and down.

Myra grabbed me as I was making my way across the room. 'Are you tight?'

'Not really tight, more tiddly.'

'What in heaven's name were you saying to Bobbie? I've never seen him like this before. He insisted on kissing my hand when he was going.'

I giggled.

'But I'm afraid Adrien is mad at me, he went off with hardly a word.'

'I think he just had a headache.'

'Anyway, I don't care, I'm enjoying myself tonight.'

With the coming of summer, the pattern of our lives began to change. Suddenly, Adrien was around much more, spending many of his evenings in the studio. Myra had explained that he was at a loose end. Many of his friends were Trinity lecturers and had gone off on the long vacation, and his mother had gone to Scotland to spend the summer with her sister. 'Adrien says she migrates every summer with the arrival of the first tripper to Greystones. Apparently it's awful there in the summer.'

Adrien often brought Bobbie along and Myra didn't seem to mind this, she seemed quite content to have the four of us spend the evening together. Sometimes she even suggested that we all go out together and we would go into town to have coffee in an hotel. I was suddenly finding myself part of a group and it was wonderful.

Mrs Harvey-Brown asked us down for a drink, sending Henry off to the pub with a billy can for ice.

'Those boys seem very keen all of a sudden.'

'Keen as mustard, Mrs Harvey-Brown.' Myra was looking at her legs, admiring her tan. She seemed much more relaxed these days, now that she had got Adrien in her setting and away from his friends. 'Of course it's Bobbie that's making the running, to be quite honest. He's really fallen for Ellen.'

'So, Ellen, are you equally keen?'

'You won't believe it, Mrs Harvey-Brown, our Ellen has turned out to be quite a *femme fatale*. Poor Bobbie doesn't know whether he's coming or going the way she's giving him the run around.'

I was used to this teasing and I liked it. It made me feel normal and part of things. As for Bobbie, well, he would never break my heart but I quite liked having him around, feeling his admiration. He made no demands on me, just hovered helpfully and admiringly. When I rose to get tea for the four of us, he always set the table. And we usually washed up together afterwards. We sometimes played cards or listened to plays on the radio. On Saturday nights Bobbie didn't come round and Adrien took Myra off, usually to the pictures.

At the beginning of July, the heat-wave began. For

three weeks the sun shone every day. The temperature rose into the eighties and people talked of nothing but their good fortune, congratulating one another as if they had arranged the whole thing. Eventually they stopped commenting and even Myra began to wish for a wisp of cloud.

The studio became impossible. We sweltered there, unable to block out the sun. By six o'clock you would actually scorch your bottom if you sat on the plastic-covered sofa. When we opened the door on our return from work, the heat detonated outwards into our faces.

'I've got it!' Myra looked up from the limp salad that she had been picking at. 'Let's move to the garden.'

'Move what?'

'Us, ninny. We can set up our summer quarters there, and stay there till it's time to go to bed.'

Henry was excited by our idea. From somewhere he produced a scythe and cut a rough lawn out of the wilderness. We brought down the fireside chairs, a card table, the bread bin and the meat safe. Myra found a huge, disused medicine chest in the bathroom and, when we had scrubbed it out, it became our crockery press. We put our butter and milk in a bucket of cold water and thrust this in the shade of the ivy-covered wall. And every evening we now spent in the open, only returning to the studio when it grew dark and the temperature had fallen.

We had picnics every night, cutting up cucumbers and tomatoes, washing crinkly heads of lettuce under the cold tap in the yard, hard-boiling our eggs on Mrs Harvey-Brown's kitchen range. We asked the Harvey-Browns to join us, but she said it was too hot and Henry was too shy to come on his own. When Adrien and Bobbie came, they often brought wine, still cool from some wine merchant's cellar. They stretched out at our feet and closed their eyes against the glare.

I had never been so happy, Myra never so affectionate. The sun eased away tensions and there seemed to be no world outside the garden, no time but the present.

Myra rubbed oil into her skin and I watched as it turned a deeper gold. I moved my fireside chair into the shade of the laburnum and protected my head further with a little cotton cap.

In the mornings we were both out of bed by seven, woken by the extraordinary brightness. The icy bathroom where we had shivered through the winter now became a pleasure room where we rushed to thrust our limbs and faces under the spurting, freezing water. At work I was filled with lassitude, moving little, talking less, blessing yet again Jack Taylor's taciturnity. I husbanded my energy for the evenings. Sometimes, at the week-ends, Adrien suggested taking us all for a trip to the sea. We thought of all those bodies and the noises and the smells and said no, no – Paradise was here, in the back garden.

It was too hot to talk. Our desensitized bodies basked like seals, demanding no more than the crunch of an apple under the teeth, the tang of lemonade at the back of the throat. We four were held, suspended in the July heat. Myra's mother wrote asking about her holiday plans but Myra could not force herself to the sticky task of penning a reply. Then, her almost forgotten cousin sent a note, inviting us both to tea. Myra told Adrien to send a telegram with our regrets that we had caught malaria or yellow fever and couldn't make it.

I had stopped thinking: my mind was white and blank, like the suddenly deserted city streets. My body, a source of so much pain over the years, now became the centre of sensuous delight as it expanded and relaxed under the benign, gold light.

Adrien lit a bonfire one night and we cooked sausages over it and drank the beer which Bobbie had brought.

The Harvey-Browns joined us and Mrs Harvey-Brown said it reminded her of summer holidays spent with her grandparents in County Cork when the country people always lit bonfires on St John's Eve. She began to cry then and Henry patted her back and Myra took her hand.

'I'm sorry,' she sniffed. 'It's absurd, I know. It's just something to do with all of you being so young and happy. I find that unbearably sad. Butterflies, pretty butterflies.'

Then Henry brought out another bottle of gin from the kitchen and she cheered up and the party went on till two o'clock in the morning.

It was towards the end of the month that the weather suddenly broke. We went to bed in the midst of a high, parched summer and awoke next morning to a sodden world. We overslept because of the unaccustomed greyness, and shivered as we searched for cardigans and raincoats and returned again and again to the window to look disbelievingly at the rain. As I was tying a headscarf under my chin, there was a knock on the door. Henry stood there in blue striped pyjamas.

'It's Mother.'

I stared at him stupidly. 'What?'

'I think she's had a stroke.'

'Oh, for heaven's sake!' Myra sounded as if she thought that this was the last straw. 'How can you tell what's wrong with her? Are you sure it's just not too much –' She bit off the gin but we both knew what she meant.

Henry was wringing his hands. 'Please come. She's all lop-sided in the bed and she can't talk or move.'

Myra turned around to give him her whole attention. 'Have you phoned the doctor?'

He shook his head.

'Right – that's the first thing to be done. Ellen, you go down with Henry and I'll go up to the kiosk. Wait till I see if I have enough pennies.'

Mrs Harvey-Brown lay in fusty twilight. I pulled back the curtains and approached the bed. She lay on her side with her mouth open and her head at a funny angle. As I watched, a thread of saliva began to slide down her chin; the turquoise ear-rings which she always wore lay on the bedside table. I walked round the bed and found myself looking into a bright, brown eye. The eye stared back at me, unblinking.

'Don't worry, the doctor's on his way, Mrs Harvey-Brown.'

There was no visible reaction.

'Can I get you anything?' I asked, unnerved by the silence. 'I mean, is there anything you want?'

For a second it seemed that the brown eye glinted more sardonically.

I sat down on the bed and forced myself to take the brown-spotted hand that lay on the counterpane. I was reminded of a childhood scene – my mother cleaning out a chicken at the kitchen table and I playing with one of its chopped-off claws. Mrs Harvey-Brown's hand felt as the claw had felt – lifeless. I raised my head and sniffed and thought I caught the high whiff of decay. There was malice in this room, an unseen third, keeping vigil with me: a jokey character on the look-out for further sport. I took out my handkerchief and wiped the spittle from Mrs Harvey-Brown's mouth.

Myra and the ambulance arrived on the doorstep together.

'Is Henry dressed?'

I nodded and stepped back to make room for the stretcher. We followed them into the bedroom and watched as they rolled Mrs Harvey-Brown onto the taut canvas.

Myra nudged Henry. 'You go with them. Come on, take off your apron, you won't need that.'

He stared at the empty bed.

'Go on. We'll look after everything here and I'll pack a bag with her nightie and stuff like that and we can take it to the hospital later. Now, off you go.'

She bundled him into the ambulance and we turned back to the house. It was dark inside and Myra began to turn lights on as she went. In the kitchen, she started opening cupboard doors at random. 'Where the hell does she keep the gin? I need a drink.'

I found an unopened bottle stashed away behind the

dinner plates on the dresser.

'Here.' Myra grabbed it and sloshed some into two tumblers. We sat and looked at the black face of the range. It was clammy in the kitchen, but cold. Outside the rain had turned into a steady downpour.

Myra refilled her tumbler. 'Jesus, the poor sod. Imagine, Ellen – this time yesterday we were complaining about the heat.' She turned to stare into the dripping garden. 'That's the end of the summer anyhow. It just shows – never depend on anything. You'd be a fool to depend on anything in this world.'

I felt I was going to cry.

Myra stood up and kicked at the empty wheelchair. 'We could clean this place up and light a fire. It might cheer up old Henry – it might even cheer us up.' She began to move back the chairs. 'Turn on the radio and see if you can get some music. And for God's sake stop looking so tragic.'

'Shut up and stop telling me what to do. I'll look tragic if I want to.'

We stared at one another, equally astonished by my revolt. Then we both started to laugh and set to work on the kitchen.

It was still raining when we set off for the hospital that evening. They had taken her to St Mary's in the Phoenix Park and we had to catch two buses to get there. We walked on either side of Henry, under the dripping trees. Over our heads the wood pigeons made mournful noises. I was carrying a bunch of pink carnations, and Henry a lemonade bottle filled with gin. We had decided that if she could drink it, she might as well have it.

Henry led the way into the ward. We walked down the middle beween two rows of old ladies, decked out in pink and white and baby blue. Mrs Harvey-Brown lay at the far end, under a picture of the Sacred Heart. She was propped up on pillows, with her hands neatly folded in front of her. She had been spruced up but she looked much the same. Nervously we sat down, looking towards the bed and then looking away again.

69

Myra was the first to speak. 'She doesn't look that bad now, does she? I mean, we didn't expect to find her up dancing a jig.'

'She's alive, Henry,' I said, 'and she's in good hands. You can rest easy at least, knowing that she's being well looked after here.'

Henry wiped his eyes with the cuff of his raincoat. 'Mother always said you were nice girls. She took a real fancy to the two of you that day you walked in.'

'You didn't know what you were letting yourself in for, did you, Mrs Harvey-Brown?'

Once Myra had addressed her, it seemed quite natural to include her in the conversation. Henry began to tell her bits of gossip and we all assured her that she was as well off here as at home, with the weather the way it was outside.

We stayed until eight o'clock when a tinny bell dismissed us. The old ladies watched us from their high, white beds as we trooped by, a different species. Outside in the park, the air smelt of earth and greenery. Henry gave the lemonade bottle to Myra. 'You might as well have it, I never touch the stuff.'

At the kitchen door we said good night and walked up the stairs towards the studio. They had never seemed so steep. The house had a different, alien feel about it. Myra made cocoa, which we hadn't had for months. Now its chocolaty warmth seemed comforting.

'I think I'll write to my mother,' Myra said. 'I haven't written in weeks.'

'Good idea.'

'In fact, I was thinking of going home for a few days. You wouldn't mind, would you, Ellen?'

'Of course not.' I could feel my desolation already.

'I hate to desert you at a time like this, you and Henry. But I'm due some leave from work and I might as well take it.'

'Don't worry about us – we'll be fine.'

And I began to wonder how we would get through the days, the hours without her.

\*     \*     \*

70

Myra had been gone five days and was not due back until Sunday. The weather had remained broken and the north wind which blew incessantly had filled the studio with unaccountable noises. I had been sleeping badly since Myra left and as a result had taken to going to bed later and later. The lack of sleep and the bad weather, but most of all Myra's absence, had left me nervy and depressed and although I had tried tonight to cheer myself up – lighting a fire and making myself some cinnamon toast – my mood had not improved.

I hated coming home from work, when the hours ahead stretched blankly. Henry's sighing presence filled the house but he had withdrawn to some hidden region where he was no longer visible. He didn't invite me down and I didn't like to knock at the kitchen door and seek him out. Adrien didn't call, which of course meant I didn't see Bobbie either. It was as if Myra in retreat had swept all the props of my life with her and had left me stranded in this high, cold room. What would it be like, I asked myself, when she was gone for good, when Adrien or some other man had finally taken her away from me? How could I survive without her presence – her egotism, her scoldings, her laughter and warmth? I could see myself in a bed-sit somewhere. Like a piece of bread I would first grow stale and then dry up completely. One day some landlady would find me and wonder whose the crumbly remains could have been.

A door banged somewhere down below, sending shivers through the house up to me in my eyrie. I couldn't stay there another minute, pretending to be cheered by a smoking fire. I threw my toast in the waste bin and, grabbing my raincoat from behind the door, fled down the stairs and out onto the streets. I was reminded of those other headlong flights from my parents' house, so different from my exit tonight. In those days I had been trying to avoid human contact; tonight I was seeking it out. I ran towards Donnybrook, searching for the busy streets. I stared into the faces of passers-by and stood close to people as they waited for buses or loitered in

71

front of shop windows. I brushed against them deliberately and listened for the comfort of their murmured conversations. When my feet refused to walk another step, I turned reluctantly to drag myself home. At least I might sleep better tonight.

As I crawled up the garden path, a figure loomed at me from the shadow of the porch.

'I'd almost given you up, so I had, but I decided to stay another while since I had stayed so long in the first place. I hope you don't mind, that it's not too late to call or anything.'

Bobbie, wonderful Bobbie!

'I was just passing and I thought I'd call, but I didn't like to disturb Henry when I saw that there was no light in the studio, so I said to myself that I'd just wait here for a while.'

'I'm delighted to see you, Bobbie. Come on up and we'll have a cup of coffee.'

I *was* delighted to see him. I thought of his bravery, the effort it must have cost him to seek me out. Had Aunt Violet raised her eyebrows and had Adrien sneered? But he had done it, he had come in from Greystones and was standing here on my doorstep. You're a person, Bobbie, I said to him now, but silently. You're not merely Adrien's cousin and I'm not merely Myra's friend. We are people in our own right.

As I spooned the coffee powder into two mugs I felt the headiness of my autonomy. I handed Bobbie his coffee and smiled at him. He smiled back. For the first time since we had met that night at the cockail party, there was affection between us. Not sexual attraction or terror or amusement or condescension but simple affection.

'Shall we go out somewhere next week?'

'Why not?'

'I mean – just the two of us?'

'As I said, why not?'

'Good then.'

I was in bondage to Myra and would remain so for as

long as she wished. I was in bondage to her because she was everything I could never be and because, by some miraculous unreason, she had chosen me. But there was another world for the ugly, the fat and the bald, where the make-dos would make do and be grateful. Tonight, as I had walked through the summer streets where the stubborn twilight lingered, I had sensed acutely the fragility of my relationship with Myra – no, not its fragility, more its fugacity. As couples sauntered past and friends walked arm-in-arm, all the exclusion of my adolescent years came rushing back, only more unbearable now that there was added to it the knowledge of loss. And, conscious once more of my oozing ugliness, I had felt that although Myra had chosen me, I could not expect the miracle to be repeated. Now here was Bobbie, shining and hairless – and human, and I knew that if I chose to reach out, he was mine. What's more, he was unlikely to be taken from me.

'We could go for a walk if the weather improves.'
'Or to the pictures if it doesn't.'
'We could do both and have coffee afterwards.'
Life was suddenly full of possibilities.

I had intended to be up to welcome Myra back on Sunday morning, but the first thing I knew she was standing over the bed, shaking me.
'I didn't expect you for hours.'
'No, I got a lift from a neighbour going to the airport.'
'How did you get in?'
'Henry answered the door, eventually. Come on, breakfast is ready down in the kitchen. I brought some lovely country eggs back with me.'
Henry gave me a sheepish look as he drew out a chair for me at the kitchen table. 'I didn't see much of you for the past week. I didn't like to disturb you.'
'And I felt the same about you.'
Myra laughed. 'You two are hopeless, I don't know what you'd do without me.'
The breakfast was delicious, rashers and eggs and a

brown cake of soda bread that Myra said some neighbour had baked for her to take back to Dublin.

'How's your mother?' Myra asked Henry, wiping the plate clean with a piece of bread.

'She's just the same, no change. The doctors told me that they don't expect any change for months. Cases like Mama's don't respond quickly, if they ever do.'

'At least it's better than a change for the worse. Henry?' She put down her knife and fork to look at him.

'Yes, Myra.'

'I've been thinking, would you mind if we started using the kitchen to cook in?'

'Why no –'

'I just thought that with your mother not here we could all eat together in the evening and it would be a lot handier for us than dragging everything upstairs. I got spoiled using the garden, I suppose.'

'I would be delighted, of course you must use the kitchen, such as it is. But you don't have to include me, you know. I don't eat much and I can –'

'Don't be daft. We'll all eat together and we can share the expenses. I like cooking, Ellen will tell you that.'

He still looked doubtful and I thought perhaps it was the memory of *Rognons Oporto*.

'If you're absolutely sure that I won't be putting you out.'

'Not another word, it's settled now.'

The new arrangement seemed to give a better balance to the house, even dissipating some of the gloom. We established a new routine with Myra and I visiting the hospital once a week and Henry going every day. He took books and read them to his mother, and brushed her hair and told her what was happening in the world. In the evenings we often sat in the drawing-room. Henry liked us to use it, saying that it had been deserted for too long.

The summer receded into normality: long chilly days, occasional bursts of sunshine ruthlessly quenched by scudding clouds. Myra put away her sun-tan lotion and I started wearing nylons again. Towards the end of

August, Myra went home for a second time, though only for the week-end.

'I'd ask you down only it's a family crisis. Daddy's hitting the bottle harder than usual and of course I have to come to the rescue. You know that pair are more like my children than my parents.'

'Give them my love.'

I didn't mind being on my own; I was even glad of the chance to get my affairs in order. I would have to call and see my own parents. I had been putting it off although father, every time he called at the office, urged me to visit home. I hadn't seen my mother since the evening I left.

On Sunday afternoon I went out. As the bus lurched across the city, I fought down the nausea which rose in my throat. With a bit of luck they might be out. But the door was opened at once.

'Ellen!' Father put his arms out. 'You're a sight for sore eyes. Come into the kitchen and see your mother.'

The kitchen was unchanged but mother looked thinner. She was sitting in her usual chair, apparently staring into space. I remembered her constant busyness when I had lived at home.

She turned and looked at me, showing no surprise. 'Hello, Ellen.' She didn't offer to kiss me or even shake hands.

Awkwardly I sat down in my old chair. 'Well, how have you been?'

'Not too bad.' Then, after a while and with what seemed tremendous effort, 'Isn't the weather terrible?'

'Terrible.'

She looked at me uncertainly. 'Would you like a cup of tea?'

She shuffled round the kitchen, eventually producing tea and shop cake, a commodity I had never known in the house. Father did the fussing, putting more coal on the fire, refilling my cup. It was as if their roles had been reversed.

She was not hostile, merely indifferent. I got the

impression of someone who was very, very tired. I drank my tea and wondered what excuse I could offer to get away.

'Keep an eye on the time, Ellen.' Mother might have read my thoughts. 'You know what the buses are like on a Sunday.'

'Well then.' I stood up. 'I suppose I'd better be off.'

She picked out a wisp of hair and began to wind it round and round a finger. Her expression was vacant and I don't think she even heard what I was saying.

'I'll just wash these up.'

'Leave them.' Father took the crockery from my hands.

'Would you both like to come to see the studio sometime? Why don't you come to tea some Sunday soon, while the summer is still with us.'

She yawned. 'Not me, Ellen, thank you all the same. I don't care to go out much these days. Your father can suit himself.'

'Maybe you'll change your mind. I'll be off then. I'll call again soon, now that the ice is broken.'

'Yes. Well, as I said, we're usually in.'

Father walked me to the bus stop.

'She's very subdued.'

He nodded. 'She's quiet enough these days, you're right there, Ellen. Do you remember the way she was always on the go? I could never find a corner to have a read in before she'd shift me out of the way with a brush or a duster. I suppose it's old age, the batteries beginning to run down. I always thought it a pity that she was never fond of reading – it's great for passing the time.'

It wasn't old age. She wasn't yet sixty but she looked a good ten years older. I was responsible for her dispirited state; when I left home I had crushed something in her.

I remembered the 13-year-old schoolgirl who had plodded off on her first day at secondary school, stiff and mountainous in her new uniform. Mother had stood at the door and waved goodbye, pride and triumph evident in every line of her body. I had hated her then for

76

not recognizing my unhappiness or, if she did recognize it, for dismissing it as childish and of no importance. Certainly not to be compared with the glory of that blazer with the school motto embroidered in Latin across the breast pocket. Poor mother, she had seemed invincible then, a force for ever in my life. Now I could hardly remember the flavour of my hatred.

I got on the bus and with each bus stop we passed my feeling of guilt grew less acute. By the time we were crossing the Liffey I felt only regret – at the waste of so much energy and passion and at my inability to be the sort of daughter she had wanted, and deserved.

I heard the radio as I began to ascend the stairs to the studio. Myra grunted at me but didn't raise her eyes from her toe-nails which she was painting a dark red.

'There!' She raised her legs in the air and began a cycling motion. 'I'm getting ready for tomorrow, it's going to be a good day.'

'Who told you that?'

'Red sky at night, the shepherd's delight. You'll see, the sun will be shining tomorrow.'

And she was right. Next day was the beginning of our Indian summer. It was wonderful, all the more so as we had stopped expecting good weather and had begun to prepare ourselves for autumn. But as we passed into September, the sun continued to shine, less hectic than in high summer but still with warmth. The mornings were magical. At the week-end we sat out on the kitchen steps and drank coffee, turning our faces upwards, taking heat from the well-baked stone. Henry had found an old panama under the stairs and he wore it now as we sat enjoying the bounty, and it seemed to me that the hat turned our mornings into tableaux so that we would be able to retrieve them in the depths of winter when their memory might bring warmth to our blood.

Adrien and Bobbie called regularly. Sometimes we all went out together, but more often now we split into couples. I preferred the joint outings, for Bobbie on his own was hard work. He had lost all his shyness with me and, as he talked freely, I grew to know him well. There was a side to him that I had not suspected, a fierce egotism beneath the timidity. Now he talked incessantly, no longer interested in my opinions, eager only for an audience. He had a great sense of grievance against the world and he liked to recount his ongoing battles to me, blow by blow. His face would grow quite crimson as he recalled a rebuff and he would jump up and down with excitement as he explained how he evened the score.

'But I soon showed him where to get off,' he'd say. 'I soon showed him that he couldn't treat me like a bit of dirt, that I wasn't going to allow myself to be walked on. So I just said to him, I said . . .'

At this stage my attention would often wander and I would grow fidgety and try to hide my yawns. When he noticed this, he would be affronted and sulk for the rest of the evening. He demanded nothing less than my glazed, unblinking stare.

And yet I was fond of him. He took me out, spent his money on me, something I had hardly expected any man to do, ever. I liked his harsh northern accent and the way he would break off a tirade to ask me if I wanted more tea or coffee, all sudden concern. He was okay and, after all, I was no great shakes.

With Myra, he remained diffident. I suppose he recognized, as I did, how far she soared above us. When we went out with the other two, we were both silent.

Myra often asked Adrien and Bobbie to Sunday dinner and the five of us, including Henry, would gather round the kitchen table. She had become an excellent cook and seemed to produce the food without effort. She enjoyed having us sit watching her as she prepared the meal, saying that she liked company while she cooked and that we mustn't dare to escape to the garden. So we drank our sherry and looked on as she stirred and chopped, a touching figure somehow in a ridiculous apron which never got dirtied. She told us jokes and made us laugh and I felt that we were all in love with her and that it was inevitable that it should be so. Then one morning I surprised an expression on Adrien's face as all other eyes were on Myra and I was sure that it was an expression of derision.

From then on I began to watch him and, as I did, I began to notice other little things. He seemed much less aware of Myra than we other three. His eyes did not follow her round the kitchen and he often didn't seem to listen to what she said. He was offhand with her, except when she tried to be serious. Then he would baby her, laugh at her and tickle her under the chin, saying wasn't his Myra such a big girl now with all these ideas rushing round in her little head?

I wondered what Myra thought or if she was aware of his behaviour. But I knew I wouldn't find out, for since that night before he had agreed to take her to the theatre, she had never discussed Adrien with me. Because of this, I had imagined that things must be going well, and then she had seemed so much more relaxed since the beginning of summer. But now I noticed the beginnings of a permanent frown between the lovely arched eyebrows.

Wretched man, I could have slapped his smirking face. I watched over Myra with more care, trying to reassure her, wishing I could tell her how far out of Adrien's ken she was. But she didn't confide in me and the barely perceptible frown remained.

As I saw Jack Taylor approaching my desk, ambling but purposeful, I thought, what have I done wrong?

It was going home time, a time when Jack never appeared. I usually shouted good night to him and his reply came through the closed door, his voice buttery with the relief of having his beloved workshop entirely to himself again. Now he stood in front of me, hopping from foot to foot. He was in such a state of embarrassment that I felt sure he must be going to give me the sack. He cleared his throat, scratched the side of his nose, then fixed his eyes on my chin.

I looked squarely at his Adam's apple. 'Did you want me for something?'

'I – Ellen?'

'Yes?' My voice squeaked from somewhere inside my head.

'I just wanted to say – it's just that – are you happy working here?'

'Very happy, very, very happy.' I was not going to make it easy for him.

'You're a good girl and I'm happy with you and I think you deserve a raise, so here we are and I don't want to hear another word about it.'

He flung the pay envelope down on my desk and scuttled off. Almost immediately the sounds of sawing and whistling started again.

I looked at the envelope, unbelieving at first. Then I slit it open and withdrew the new, sweet-smelling notes. There were two extra. One would have been generous, two was munificent, far more than I felt I was worth. Dear, kind Jack. I wondered what I would do with such wealth. Already I was able to save something every week, now I could see myself amassing a fortune.

I would have a celebration dinner tonight, I decided, a surprise for Myra and Henry. Myra was working late and Henry was at the hospital, so with a bit of luck I'd have it on the table before either of them came home.

'Good night Jack and thanks very much,' I called as I pulled the cover down on my typewriter. The whistling behind the partition increased in volume as the sawing increased in speed.

The shops in Donnybrook were crowded when I got there. We didn't usually shop in the neighbourhood as Myra said they were all robbers, catering for the people who still lived in big houses around. Now, fingering my pay envelope, I moved nonchalantly from shop to shop. I bought a fat chicken, some celery with feathery green leaves and a bottle of pink wine from Portugal. I was drawn by the smell to a small bakery where I chose six little glazed apricot tarts and a carton of cream to go with them. Finally I got a cigar for Henry – he liked to smoke one on a special occasion when he donned what he called his smoking jacket. I gathered my purchases together and squeezed my pay packet. Still plump.

I hurried down the road, planning the table decorations, wondering if I could find a flower anywhere in the overgrown garden. At our house I left the path and crossed to the side entrance. We came in this way now, since we had started to share the kitchen with Henry – round the side of the house, through the back yard and in the back door. It was much handier, particularly when one or other of us was carrying shopping as I was now.

I pushed in the gate of the side entrance and, as I did, I paused. Light from the uncurtained kitchen window was reflected onto the roughly cut grass. Was somebody there? Neither Myra nor Henry could be home this early, so – I shivered. The garden, full of the shadows of a waning twilight, seemed suddenly full of menace. And burglars surprised at work could turn very nasty. Cautiously, I began to inch forward towards the light. I laid my packages against the wall of the house and crawled along until I reached the sill of the kitchen window. I began to raise my head, slowly, my eyes shut tight in fear of what I might see inside. But – was that the radio playing dance music? Funny sort of burglar to turn on a radio.

The kitchen shone in front of me, new minted. The range glowed, the mugs on the dresser sparkled. Two people sat at the table, the radio between them. I squinted to bring them into focus; Myra and Bobbie. I laughed outright, a mixture of relief and surprise. No burglars then, but what were these two doing here? Had Myra got off early from work and why was Bobbie here at all? It wasn't his evening for calling round and anyway he would never have come so early. It was as if I had come upon a secret rendezvous. I laughed again at the absurdity of such an idea.

I could not take my eyes from the scene in front of me. I was reminded of my night walks when I had sometimes come across uncurtained windows and had stood staring in fascination at the glimpse into another life. Now, although I knew these two, looking in from the dank garden I still felt some of that magic.

But what were they doing? I watched their lips moving, unable to hear what they said because of the radio. They were drinking something, sherry I thought from the colour, and laughing across the table at each other. Perhaps Myra *had* got off early from the library, though that in itself was unusual, but I could think of no reason why Bobbie should be sitting there. He would have known I wouldn't be home, and anyway he never called round, like that, casually. We had a date for the following Sunday, so what was he doing here tonight?

The music from the radio changed and Myra's arm reached out to turn off the sound. What was I going to do about my special dinner – my plans were ruined. The surprise of seeing those two together had put it right out of my head, but now I realized that I would hardly have enough food for Bobbie as well as the three of us and I could hardly not ask him to stay.

Myra's laugh drew my attention back. She was sitting now with her chin in her hand, gazing at Bobbie as if he were the most fascinating specimen of manhood. Her lips were slighty parted, her eyes large and unblinking.

'I've always been like that so I have,' Bobbie was saying. 'I suppose it's because I'm a bit on the small side. Aunt Violet used to say that the weedy stage would pass but I'm afraid –'

Myra stopped him by placing a hand in front of his mouth. 'I won't hear you talk like that, Bobbie, you're every bit as attractive in your own way as Adrien. I mean, it would be a very boring world if everyone looked the same and offered the same talents, wouldn't it now?'

Bobbie's voice sounded in his throat like a purr. If I watched any longer, I thought, he'll start licking her.

I turned towards the garden in sudden understanding. It *was* a rendezvous after all, that must be the explanation. She had been giving him the full treatment, head thrown back, lips moistened. But how could she desire him, his pink, simpering face? How could she have designs on that? I knew he was hers if she beckoned, but she couldn't want him. And besides, to betray me? No, never that. Then why? Why the meeting, why the seductive voice, the hand lifted tenderly to his mouth? Did she perhaps realize that Adrien's interest was cooling? After all, I had noticed it myself and –

At the scrape of the kitchen door, I fled to the coal shed. I listened to the fall of their voices and the warm flavour of their goodbyes. Bobbie's shoes sparked along the flagged path to the side entrance.

I reached out a hand to steady myself. My head. Someone had begun to hammer a nail through the bones of my skull, pound, pound. I shook my head and shook it, but they wouldn't stop. I staggered into the garden and over to the house. On the threshold I stopped and pushed the door open. A figure at the sink turned towards me. 'Hiya, Ellen!'

At first I could not see who it was – everything before me remained blurred. Then the beautiful face snapped into focus. I thought of how much I had loved her, how dear she had been to me. And to be betrayed for an idiot man.

'I've been entertaining your beau,' nastily said. The lips sneered, the eyes glittered with malice.

A pulse began to beat at the base of my neck and I felt as if my face was on fire as blood rushed upward from every part of my body. I lunged across the kitchen towards her, to shake her, to make her explain to me, to find sense somewhere. But she stood, one hand resting on the table, an ankle crossed over the other. I could feel the arrogance of her body. Her fingers beat out a tattoo: so what are you going to do now, what now? Inches from the hand, the blade of the breadknife winked at me in the light of the overhead bulb. I grabbed it and lunged once more.

I was surprised by the lack of resistance to the knife, just a squelchy sound, like a foot inside a wet shoe. Then I released my grip and Myra crashed backwards onto the floor.

83

I looked at the scene before me and it didn't seem real. The corpse lay on the floor under the glare of the overhead light, the only noise coming from the range where the fire coughed and snorted.

It couldn't be, Myra wasn't dead, that brown stuff on the front of her jumper was certainly not blood. It was a play, a scene from a film.

As I moved forward, I found my body suddenly weightless. I looked at my hands stretched in front of me like a sleep-walker's. They weren't real, at least they didn't seem to belong to me. And yet, with this disorientation I felt a surge of capableness, as if I could do anything. I began to busy myself, to get rid of the evidence.

'Don't move or even twitch, Myra, or you'll spoil the effect,' I warned, skirting her to reach the table where her purse, a brown leather wallet, lay. I took it up, emptied the coins into my pocket and squeezed it through the bars of the range. With the poker I thrust it far into the heart of the fire and within seconds it was unrecognizable. I turned back to the room and began to open drawers and cupboards at random. Objects fell onto the floor, and for good measure I overturned two chairs. I watched myself, my hands creating the chaos, and thought what a good job I was making of it.

There was something else they always did at this stage – what was it? Fingerprints, I must get rid of fingerprints. I knelt beside her and stretched out my hand to rub the shaft of the knife with my handkerchief. Up and down I polished, up and down, but my fingers

recoiled from something – something jammy and warm.
I looked down . . . brown, horrible . . .

Someone was screaming. The high, thin sound filled
the kitchen, bouncing back off the brown-painted walls.
I was standing up, my hands by my side – the noise was
becoming intolerable. I felt a pressure on my shoulders
as someone grabbed me from behind. Then I found
myself being shaken, so roughly that my head began to
bounce up and down. I clamped my mouth shut. The
screaming stopped.

Arms encircled me now and I was drawn onto a bosom
which smelled of soap and turf smoke.

'Hush,' a voice said and then, 'I'll take her home,
Henry, you get the guards.'

Henry. I raised my head and there he was, his hands
fluttering up and down in distress. Then what about my
dinner, my surprise dinner and where was –?

'Don't, please Ellen, don't. You're all right now, Mrs
Earley will take you home next door with her and everything will be all right.'

I knew that wasn't true, never again could everything
be all right. Never.

But the woman was shunting me out, making little
soothing noises. I was glad then to be going with her, to
be leaving all the rest behind. She seemed so strong. I
grasped her hand and, closing my eyes, allowed myself
to be led out.

I stumbled down the path behind her. It was cold and
my teeth were rattling in my head, I couldn't stop the
chattering.

'Come on, into the sitting-room with you. Wasn't it a
mercy I had the electric fire on and the place nice and
warm. Now you just sit down and I'll get you a nice cup
of tea.'

This was better. I looked around the room with a sense
of relief. It was just like our front room at home, small
and crowded. There were photographs and ornaments
and brightly coloured cushions. There were furry rugs
on the floor and flowers in full bloom on the walls. Every

corner was shining and polished; every squarely placed ornament part of Mrs Earley's deliberate design. I was all right here for I knew that nothing could happen in this room without her permission.

'Here you are, love.'

The tea was sweet and strong, the way I liked it. I hoped she would offer me another cup and then I would like to sleep. I could sleep for a month, I had never known such exhaustion.

But there was a knocking now, somewhere outside the little room. Mrs Earley shook her head but it came again.

'Never you mind,' she said, 'I'll send them off with a flea in their ear.'

But she didn't. She came back with two men, tall, in dark suits. They smiled at me with yellow teeth and sat down, crowding round the electric fire. The older one leant towards me and I smelt onion on his breath.

'Now Miss Yates – it *is* Miss Yates?'

I nodded.

'We just want you to answer a few questions. We'll be as quick as possible, we know what you've been through already.'

Mrs Earley had come to sit on the arm of my chair and was making clucking noises at the man.

'Are you ready then, Miss?'

I began to tremble. He was asking me to think about something horrible, something which I had been keeping out of my mind, buried. It was awful and I knew I couldn't even allow myself to recall it. But then I remembered that was the way it always happened in a film. The detectives always called and questioned.

I turned and nodded at the man.

'Well then, if you could just tell me in your own words everything that happened tonight. Start from the time you left work. Did you come home at the usual time and did you expect to find anyone there? What was the usual timetable for a Friday night? I mean, for example, Miss Boland usually worked late, didn't she?'

I began to speak. I must concentrate on my voice, that

was the important thing. I must pay attention to the way I said things. And the expression on my face had to be right and the lines of my body. It was all the little details that made acting convincing.

I was good, I know I was good. They never took their eyes off my face, even Mrs Earley seemed spellbound. They only had to ask me one or two questions, otherwise I told them everything simply and with clarity. I could tell quite clearly that they appreciated the fact that I was making so little fuss. When I came to describe the scene in the kitchen, I just closed my eyes and got through it quickly.

They stayed about an hour and when they had gone Mrs Earley plumped up the cushions that they had flattened and opened the window a crack. She smiled at me. 'That's that then and good riddance to bad rubbish.' She took my hand. 'And now it's bed for you. I'm putting you in my girls' room and I'll be sleeping in the other bed. My girls have gone off, ten years now in Manchester, but I keep the beds made up, and look now how they've come in handy. And I'll be there if you want anything.'

When I awoke I knew at once that I wasn't in the studio because of the lack of light. I turned towards the night, looking for the stars, but there were none, no gradation in the dark even, just a dense, furry black. I could feel it encircling me, entombing me. I sat up abruptly, banging my head against something.

I blinked in the flush of light.

'Isn't it just as well I'm a light sleeper?' Mrs Earley was sitting up in the other bed. She pulled a cardigan onto her shoulders and came over to me.

'Was it a bad dream, love?'

Oh, if only it had been that. But now I knew, I knew that it was real, it had happened. I clutched her hand. 'I didn't mean to do it, Mrs Earley, I never meant to, how could I when I loved her so much? It was just the knife, I saw the knife winking at me . . . And then the blood on my hand, like jam.'

She drew my head onto her shoulder so that my mouth was stopped by her cardigan. 'Hush and don't talk such nonsense. You've been having a nightmare, which isn't surprising I suppose, considering everything. But no more talk about winking knives and such like rubbish. Your poor friend was killed by some robber, but you don't need to think about that. You must just think that her troubles are over now, she's with Jesus now, not like the rest of us creatures still in this vale of tears.'

'But Mrs Earley –'

'No more buts.' She forced my head down again and began to rock me like a baby. 'I've some warm milk in a flask over there, the best thing for getting you off to sleep. I'll give you a sup and the next thing you know it'll be the morning.'

I drank my milk and lay down. Mrs Earley turned out the light but opened the door so that the landing bulb shone in. I raised my hands before my face and began to look at them. They were nice hands, delicate, with long fingers and pretty nails, now that I had stopped biting them. They were my only good feature and I had been proud of them, secretly. Had they really taken that knife – had they plunged it . . .? It didn't seem possible, soft, white things. Perhaps Mrs Earley was right after all, perhaps it had all been a nightmare.

But she was dead. Myra was dead.

I said the words to myself and, as I did, I realized how unimportant it was who had killed her or how she had died. She was dead. I would never see her again, I would never hear her speak. She was undone, unmade, gone.

It was so ludicrous that I began to laugh. So much vitality, so much energy and passion couldn't just be extinguished like that. For ever. Snuffed out, blown away like so much dust. Dust thou art and unto dust thou shalt return. But I rebelled at that. Myra had not been so much dust. She had been colour and light and movement. She had been life itself.

And she was dead.

The pain, starting in my chest, flooded through the

rest of my body. The varying bits of me lost their identity as they became caught up in its rage. But, as I gritted my teeth and then could no longer feel them, I held onto the hope that if this continued till morning, I too might die.

But I was alive next morning to see the dawn's streaky light struggling through Mrs Earley's flimsy curtains. I must have dozed off then, for the next thing I became conscious of was someone shaking me, gently.

'Your mammy's here, love. She's come to take you home. Henry went off this morning to get her, he thought you needed a mother at a time like this.'

Mother was dressed in her visiting best – matching hat and coat, black leather gloves and bag.

'My darling child,' she said and flung her arms around me. Father stood at the door, flicking imaginary specks of dandruff from his shoulders.

They treated me like someone in the last stages of a fatal illness. They had kept a taxi waiting and I was driven home, all the way across the city, in its fat, comfortable interior. Then they put me to bed with a hot water bottle and mother made blancmange, as she had always done during childhood illnesses. I looked round my little room, cold and pale as I remembered it. The walls were a faded blue, the light filtering through the lace curtain grey and steady. I closed my eyes and turned my back on it. But it was still there when I awoke. This had been my adolescent refuge and bolt-hole, and yet the place that had emphasized and defined my loneliness. Nobody has ever suffered like this, I used to think, nobody could endure such pain. Now I realized that my suffering was over – I had passed from suffering to despair. While I suffered I had hoped. Why, I had even prayed in those days – please God, make me thin and I'll never eat another chocolate biscuit for the rest of my life. Please God, please, let me have just one friend.

What would I pray for now, even if there was anyone to pray to?

\*　　\*　　\*

89

I stayed one week and every moment made me realize more clearly what it was I had destroyed. The girl who had inhabited this house had been part of an order. Her own life had been a jumble perhaps, but there had been a world outside of her where good and evil existed, where the sun rose in the morning and went down at night. That was all gone now, all that remained was chaos.

So I kissed mother goodbye and promised that I would keep in touch. I would be safe at Mrs Earley's, and anyway lightning never strikes twice in the same place. It was she who said this, doubtfully, as she followed me down the path. She was too worried about my safety, I could see, to be annoyed at this, my second desertion of the nest.

The police called the day I arrived back and asked me all the same questions. Then they came again two days later and we went through it all once more. They told me that the inquest was to take place at the end of the month and I would be called to give evidence.

I almost enjoyed my battle with the guards, the feeling that I was outwitting them; it became a game. I don't think I was trying to save my own skin, not consciously anyhow, nor did I now see myself playing a scene from a film. One day after they had gone I thought – why don't I just tell them the truth and have it all over and done with? But I knew I couldn't, I couldn't do that to her memory. I thought of the speculation if it all came out: the newspaper stories and innuendoes and whisperings. Had she been that sort of girl, stealing other people's boyfriends? Had she been in the habit of entertaining men on her own, offering them alcohol in a deserted house? And who would believe me if I had protested that this was not so? Then, why had I killed her? I could never explain those few seconds that had destroyed two lives. I didn't know myself how it had happened, how that slack white hand had suddenly, of its own accord, raised the knife and plunged.

Myra's body lay buried in the yellow Sligo clay. The

90

flesh would stink by now as it began to disintegrate in chunks. Something had to remain intact.

So I fought the guards. At the inquest I spoke up, so as not to irritate the coroner. I realized also that I was not the only one who had been lying. Bobbie was there but he was not called as a witness. He had obviously not told the guards about his visit that night. Nothing suspicious in this I knew, just sheer cowardice. I looked at his sweating, hairless face and thought how I should have killed him. If he had stayed in the North, none of this would have happened. It was really his fault.

I had not seen him since that night I had gazed on him through the kitchen window. Neither he nor Adrien had called round but now, as I left the room where the inquest had been held, he made a half-hearted attempt to approach me. I looked at him, squarely, hoping that he could read my contempt, and then I deliberately turned away. As he walked down the corridor I could sense the relief in every spindly step.

Adrien, whom I had seen inside with his mother, crossed over to speak to Henry. I scuttled off in case I should be drawn into the conversation. I certainly had nothing to say to him. As I waited for Henry, the Bolands came out. They were both weeping and, as they passed me by, Mrs Boland reached out and touched my cheek. I began to weep then, useless tears. They were helped into a car by a priest, a big, black car, like a hearse. I wondered where Mrs Boland got the black coat she wore, it was obviously not hers, too dowdy and countrified. I imagined some neighbour buttoning her into it, as she stood, helpless, waiting for the journey to Dublin. What was to become of them now that Myra was no longer there?

I never saw them again.

For two weeks, Henry and I stayed in Mrs Earley's house. Henry slept in the spare room and I shared her daughters' room with Mrs Earley. Mr Earley snored peacefully in the front bedroom. Mrs Earley still mourned the loss of her daughters. She filled the empty drawers in their room with lavender and rosemary and she left the pictures of singers and film stars up on the walls. I used to examine them every morning, their dated hair-styles and dress. I wondered about the girls who had stuck them there and what had driven them from this room with its pink-frilled dressing table and scented air.

Henry was settling in, burrowing a permanent niche for himself, I could see.

'We can't stay here for ever, Henry,' I said one night, as we did the washing-up together.

He sighed. 'I suppose not, but it's such a dear little house, so cosy. I remember when they built this terrace, twenty years ago, I wanted Mother to buy one of the houses and sell ours. I thought it would be just right for the two of us, easy to clean and keep warm. Do you notice how warm it is?'

I did, and how thin the walls were. I knew about that sort of house, I had been brought up in one. I knew that if you pulled the lavatory chain the walls shook, and that if you coughed you were liable to bring a fall of soot down the chimney.

'We can't stay here, Henry. It wouldn't be fair to Mrs Earley.'

He looked wistful. 'I suppose not.'

'Don't you want to get back to your own house?'

'No.'

'Are you nervous about going back – I mean, after what happened?'

He gave an embarrassed giggle. 'I know it's silly but I can't help dwelling on it. I'd feel peculiar settling back in there as if nothing had happened.'

'I'd be with you.'

But he shook his head.

The next evening Mrs Earley said at tea, 'Get it blessed, Henry.'

Henry stared at her. 'Mrs Earley?'

'I said you should get that place of yours blessed. I was passing by just now and I was having a look at it and you can't just leave it there, you know. I mean, it'll fall down if you leave it without any heating much longer. Them big old houses are full of damp, and I was noticing the way you never go near it. I suppose it's natural that you'd feel queer about it after what happened but you should look after it.'

Henry nodded. 'I've been meaning to talk to you about that, Mrs Earley. I know we can't stay here indefinitely.'

'Well, you can and welcome, and I wasn't trying to hint that it was time you were leaving. You're great company for me but that house of yours needs seeing to.'

'I have been worrying about it and I have had reservations about going back.'

'That's it then, you'll feel differently about it if you get it blessed. Do they do that sort of thing in your Church?'

'I'm sure they do.'

'Right then, get in the vicar and your troubles are over.'

We moved back on a Saturday. I was to have a small back bedroom over the kitchen, the warmest room in the house according to Henry. I put my shoes under the bed and my skirts in the wardrobe and once more hung my raincoat on its hook in the hall. It didn't seem strange to be back, just natural. Living in Mrs Earley's house my life had been suspended. After the first few days of pain, I had stopped feeling anything. I had been in a state of catalepsy, watching even the gravel being shovelled onto the coffin without any sensation. Now, however, my period of mourning began. Now, back in the world that I had shared with her, I felt Myra's loss like hunger. At night I walked the floor, back and forth, seeking distraction in the monotony of the movement. In the morning I faced Henry with red, sore eyes. One morning he suggested tentatively that I should perhaps see a doctor or go back to my parents again until I was feeling better. But I said no, it will pass.

And it did. When I said it to Henry, I hadn't really believed that it would, that the pain would ever grow less intense. But now, after about two months, it was beginning to. I started to sleep again and eventually I could accept quite calmly the fact that Myra was gone. I was left with only one permanent disability – I had lost my taste for life. It was like having a cold without being really sick. There was no longer any fever, there was even a certain inclination to eat, but the food, when placed on the tongue, tasted like sawdust. All of my world had become a sawdust world.

But this was not altogether unpleasant. An absence of joy meant also an absence of pain; a blunting of sensations meant an increase in calm. This must be what it's like to be very old, I thought; a grey-tinted sky viewed from a steady ocean as one waited patiently for death.

Henry was my anchor. With him I began my new life and from him I sought shelter. When he told me he was thinking of bringing his mother home, I was delighted.

'Mrs Earley suggested it – I hadn't thought of it, but she said it wasn't proper you and me here alone together. I mean, your good name and you know the way people talk. Shall we manage her between us, do you think? I'm sure she wants to come home.'

'Of course we'll manage her, it will be no trouble.'

I had to smile at Henry's preoccupation with propriety but I thought also that with Mrs Harvey-Brown back at home there was less likelihood of Henry growing restless and wanting to sell.

She came in an ambulance and two men carried her into what had been the dining-room when Henry's father was alive. It was next door to the kitchen and so would make the fetching and carrying easier.

'Anyway, we'll see how it goes,' Henry said on the first night as I prepared her food. 'We'll see how well we can manage.'

I sat on the bed while Henry fed her. We had tried to brighten up the room with new curtains and a bright blue bedspread, but none of these frivolities distracted

94

the eye from the shrivelling bundle in the bed.

'It's nice having Mother home, isn't it? I mean, apart from other considerations, I'm glad she's back, it's nice.'

She began to splutter and he raised her up, gently clapping her between the shoulders. His touch was sure and deft.

'You should have married, Henry.'

He smiled. 'As if anyone would have me.'

And he wiped his mother's mouth and laid her back on the pillows.

I felt something then, not for myself but for the blighted lives around me. We closed the door on the drooling noises and tiptoed to the kitchen.

Every second Sunday now I crossed the city to my parents' house. I had become a sort of local celebrity, for even if the circumstances had not been the conventional ones, I had had my photograph in the paper. The neighbours eyed me speculatively as I walked down the road or engaged me in conversations which always got round to the one subject that interested them where I was concerned. They enjoyed this brush with danger and I indulged their mild ghoulishness. Mother smiled and nodded and encouraged me to talk. In some strange fashion she seemed to find reflected glory from my notoriety.

The visits were never long as both she and my father worried about my being out late. They thought I was still staying with Mrs Earley and they questioned me about the locks on the doors and whether Mr Earley ever slept away from home. I hadn't told them of my return to the Harvey-Browns' – they would have been horrified to know I was back living at the scene of the crime and certainly would not have considered a bedridden old lady to be of any use as a chaperone.

Once more, mother had begun to interest herself in my life. 'How are the boyfriends, then?' It was the standard question.

'The same as last time – non-existent.'

'Well, it won't be long now, for you're turning into quite a handsome girl. Though, of course, handsome is as handsome does.'

She was right and not merely seeing me with a mother's ever hopeful eyes – my appearance *was* improving. For no reason I had begun to lose weight and my skin had begun to clear as well. I was made aware of these changes by the reaction of the men around me. It was as if I had suddenly become visible. The butcher no longer overlooked me as I queued patiently for my meat; the bus conductor took my fare the first time round. But when a man smiled at me, when his eyes said 'I fancy you', I wanted to push his silly face in. It was too late for all that now and the farther men steered clear of me, the better pleased I was.

The routine, the monotony of my life made it bearable. There was the fortnightly visit to my parents, my unchanging and undemanding job and my evenings spent with Henry. Throughout the day I looked forward to those evenings when Henry and I would pull up our chairs to the range and switch on the radio. We took turns reading the evening paper and I usually had bits of sewing to do. If there had been an accident with Mrs Harvey-Brown I might have some extra washing. At ten o'clock I made the cocoa and by half-past ten I was in bed. I listened for Henry, his footsteps, and the opening and closing of his door. Then there was just the dark to be got through as the house settled down for the night. I slept with my light on, but I did sleep. And when I awoke there was no longer that awful moment when I thought things were as they had been. Now, with the return of consciousness came the immediate recognition of the present. I grasped at my shrunken world and thought, yes, if it stays like this I can endure it.

So when the knock came at the door one evening, I was frightened. Nobody ever called at this time. Mrs Earley, who was our only visitor, always came before tea.

'I'd better see who it is.' Henry pushed back his chair.

At first I didn't know him, as he stood in the doorway,

96

his face elusive but familiar in the manner of film stars.

'Hello, Ellen, how are you? I was just in the neighbourhood so I thought I'd look in and see how you were.'

'Hello, Adrien.'

'I was glad to hear Mrs Harvey-Brown was back with you. It must be –'

He stopped abruptly as his eyes left my face and slid towards the red tiles of the floor. Some of the pinkness left his cheeks and he swallowed hard.

I sniggered. 'We've had the place blessed so you needn't worry.'

'Oh.' For a moment he seemed thrown by my crassness but then he recovered and settled himself manfully in Henry's chair. I hated him and his casual assumption that he could re-enter our lives like this.

'I'm not interrupting anything, I hope?'

'Not a thing. We weren't doing anything special this evening, were we, Ellen?'

I glared at them both.

'I've – I haven't been getting around much in the past few months, pressures at work, you know.'

Henry nodded wisely.

'But I have often wondered how you were getting on since – I mean. Well, I just hoped that everything was okay.'

'That was kind of you, Adrien. We've been fine, haven't we, Ellen? It is nice to have Mother back even though it means extra work for Ellen, but then she's very kind too. I've got very kind friends.'

'We've all been through something together' – seriousness had made Adrien's features loutish – 'and I think that an experience like we've been through forms some sort of bond, don't you?'

I felt I couldn't take any more of this nonsense. I stood up.

'Excuse me, will you, I've things I must do upstairs.'

As I huddled in my bedroom, I wondered really why he had called. I didn't believe for a moment that he had been worrying about our well-being, or that he ever gave

97

us a thought – probably he had just found himself at a loose end and decided to go slumming. Whatever it was, I wanted none of it. Anyway, he had ruined my evening.

I was still huddled on my bed when there was a timid knock on my door.

'It's me, Ellen. I've made us some cocoa.'

'Has he gone?'

'Yes.'

I opened the door. 'I'll come down then.'

The cocoa was warm and reassuring. This is the way my evenings always ended, this was what I wanted to continue.

Henry cleared his throat. 'Adrien is afraid he upset you.'

'Whatever gave him that idea?'

'He should have realized – we both should have, that the visit, his presence would bring everything back to you.'

I looked at him, astonished. The visit brought nothing back. That was finished, buried, over and done with. Adrien's delayed sensitivity was misplaced. I just didn't want him blundering into my world, that was all.

'He's had a hard time too.'

'Has he?'

'I'm sorry, I should have realized that this would upset you.'

'Look, Henry – I'm not upset, I just don't have much to say to Adrien. I don't care if he comes here – it'd be very cheeky of me to start telling you who you could invite to your own house. But I don't want to have to entertain him, that's all.'

Henry said nothing for some seconds as we both gazed at the fire in the range. Then, 'Ellen.'

'Yes?'

'I've been a bit worried about you lately, the fact that you never go out. It's all right for an old fogy like me, but you're too young not to have a life of your own. It's not much fun, just being here with Mother and me, not very exciting.'

98

'Henry – you sound just like my mother. Look, I'm perfectly all right the way I am – I like my life. You mustn't bully me, Henry, into leading the kind of life you think I might enjoy. I'm all right the way I am, really, you must believe me.'

He continued to cluck but he agreed that I might be quite content, odd though that might appear to outsiders. Then, as I was washing the mugs and he was damping down the fire, he said, 'I suppose you know about Bobbie?'

'Know what?'

'He's gone back up North. He went when his course finished – Adrien told me – about a fortnight ago.'

I laughed outright. 'I won't be losing any sleep over that so you can stop looking so woebegone.'

At least *he* wouldn't be finding himself in the neighbourhood.

I was more prepared for his second visit, though I couldn't escape this time for I was baking bread when he arrived. But at least I didn't have to sit in a cosy circle round the range; I was busy at the table. I studied the back of Adrien's head, wondering again why he was seeking us out. He was a well-set-up man inside his tweed jacket, he had money and a sports car, and yet here he was spending a Saturday night in this kitchen with the two of us. He had even brought a present, a pot-plant for Mrs Harvey-Brown. I never remembered him doing anything like that before, when he had sat in our midst in the old days and we had woven anxious circles round him, anticipating his needs and his moods.

He moved his chair back from the heat so that now I could see his profile. He had been considered good-looking; even Mrs Harvey-Brown, whose standards in male attractiveness were very high, had said so. Any time I had dared to raise my eyes to his face, I had concurred. But there was a change in him. The air of assurance had gone, the sheen of self-confidence. The eyes didn't quite meet yours, the mouth apologized. The face that presented itself was dull and ordinary, nothing special any more.

And to think that I had trembled in his presence, blushed when I heard his foot on the stairs. Remembering the effect that men had on me in that other world made me feel almost nostalgic now.

He turned his head suddenly and caught me staring at him. He held my gaze and said, 'I was thinking of going for a drive somewhere tomorrow, getting out of the city. Would either of you care to come?'

'You go.' Henry and I spoke together.

'Well, don't all rush.'

'I'll mind your mother, Henry, you need an outing.' We all three knew that the invitation had really been intended for me but I was determined to ignore this. They stared at me while I smiled encouragement at Henry.

Suddenly, he returned the smile. 'I've got it – we'll both go. Mrs Earley will mind Mother for a couple of hours and we can both take advantage of your kind offer, Adrien. Can you squeeze us both in?'

In spite of myself I enjoyed the outing. During the night, I had thought about not going; I could feign sickness or simply say I didn't want to go out anywhere in that silly little car. But although I didn't give a damn about Adrien, I knew Henry would be upset, on everyone's behalf. So although I was still cross with him for out-manoeuvring me, I went.

Henry sat in the middle where he was getting squashed, I hoped. I stared out the window and Adrien sped us along to Howth. The roads were empty, it was too early in the year for seaside trippers. I remembered that the last time I had been out here had been with my father. I had been ten and we had taken a picnic and he had talked to me about outings with his father, my grandfather, whom I had never known.

It was cold in Howth, with a strong wind off the sea.

'I'll just wander off for a bit by myself, if you don't

mind,' I said, getting out of the car and scurrying off before they could make an attempt to join me.

I began to climb the hill in the teeth of the wind. The gradient was quite steep but I was glad of the effort demanded of my under-exercised body. Soon, I was no longer noticing the bite of the wind.

The summit was deserted, as was the sea down below. Even the seagulls had stayed at home. I wasn't used to this sort of air and I felt light-headed. I lay on the spiky grass and peered downwards. The world expanded, spinning away from me, and I could feel a wrenching apart of the many strictures and tightnesses around my soul. If I cast myself off this hill I was sure I would fly. My body, stretched on the turf, felt weightless, so complete was the sense of ease which encompassed it.

I recognized it instantly, the taste of happiness. Then it was gone and I was plodding downhill, my face and hands sore from the cold.

Half-way down, the men came into view. They were walking up and down in front of Adrien's car, both with their coat collars turned up.

'We were thinking of going for a drink,' Adrien said.

'Off you go then, I'll wait for you in the shelter here.'

'But you must come with us. We'll go to a hotel and you can have tea or coffee if you'd prefer.'

I did feel like a cup of tea and a hotel lounge seemed preferable to a windy shelter. Henry took my arm and we followed Adrien along a broken pavement through a sleeping town.

The hotel was deserted. By the look of it, it might have been like this for years. We walked along a dark corridor, past an empty dining-room and a closed bar to a room marked Tea Lounge. This, too, was empty. We chose not to sit by the smoky fire but in the bay window where we could look out on the grey and shining sea. A giant radiator gurgled but gave off little heat.

'This is ridiculous,' said Adrien. 'There isn't even a bell one can ring.' And he went off in search of someone.

I was delighted with all the gothic gloom.

After another five minutes an elderly waitress came in and stared at us in surprise. 'Were you wanting something?'

'Well of course we were,' Adrien said crossly. 'We'd like some tea and –'

'We don't do teas.'

'Coffee then.'

'No coffee neither.'

'For heaven's sake! What *do* you do?'

'You can have a drink or a mineral.'

The drinks arrived in sticky glasses and the waitress slopped some of them as she placed them on the table. She glared at Adrien, daring him to say a word.

'I'm sorry,' he said as she flounced out.

'It doesn't matter and it's not your fault anyway.'

'No, but I'm sure Ellen would have liked tea.'

Clearly, he saw the afternoon spoiled. He gulped his drink and hurried us from the lounge. On the way home, he didn't speak. He must have had expectations beyond mine of the afternoon outing.

'I'm sorry it was such a disaster,' he apologized again as we got out of the car.

'I enjoyed myself,' I said and was surprised to realize that I had.

'And so did I, Adrien, it was a jolly nice trip.'

'We might do it again sometime.'

Adrien gaped at me. 'Do you mean it?'

'Yes.'

And, strangely, I did. I felt no differently about Adrien. As far as my life was concerned, he could play no part in it. But it *had* been nice to get out of the city and I had hardly noticed Adrien during the afternoon. If for some reason which I could not comprehend he wanted to drive me on such outings in his little car, then I might as well take advantage of his strange desire.

Mother looked at me with the sort of long-suffering expression that had grown familiar to me over the years. Now that she had begun to interest herself in my

102

life again, all her old bustle and plump self-confidence had returned. This Sunday afternoon, searching for something to talk about, I had foolishly mentioned my trip to Howth. I should have known that she would react as she was now doing.

'Why do you always slouch?' she said, and added, 'I think it is most peculiar, you going out on a date with him.'

'But it wasn't a date.'

'What was it then?'

'Henry was there too.'

'Yes, but you said he's asked you out on your own next week.'

'Yes, but –'

'There you are then. No, it's just not right, Ellen. I mean, you wouldn't think he'd want to in the circumstances – now would you? I'd be careful of that fellow if I were you. Oh, laugh away, but they never found out who did it and I do think his behaviour is most queer. The world is full of dangerous people, I shouldn't have to tell you that. Where is he taking you?'

'For a drive somewhere.'

'Just look at that. If you must go out, why don't you go to the pictures where there would be lots of people, not off in a car, God knows where. I can't understand you, Ellen, I really can't. You'd think you'd have had your warning but you just won't learn.'

Poor mother. I wondered what her reaction would be if I told her why I knew I had no reason to fear Adrien. Of course, I also think that she worried about the lack of taste I was displaying, my indelicacy in going out with him at all.

As for me, these trips were made possible by the fact that I didn't have to bother about Adrien. Although I hadn't told her, we had already been out together on our own and it was like being driven by a chauffeur. We hardly spoke, and when we did, it was impersonal and polite. It wouldn't worry me if tomorrow he stopped taking me out, but in the meantime it was a pleasant diversion.

103

On the next Sunday I sat into the car as if I had been doing it all my life. He said, 'We're going somewhere a bit unusual, somewhere I hope you'll like.'

We skirted the Phoenix Park and I thought we should have given Henry a lift to the hospital, before I remembered that Mrs Harvey-Brown was now at home with us. Soon we had left the city behind and were out on a road I did not know. The trees on either side gave way to demesne walls and then they appeared again. I felt the dullness, the claustrophobia of high hedges. Then the vista opened somewhat and I thought we must be heading for the midlands as I looked out at the flat countryside, field after field of grazing land. There were few houses, just some ugly cottages every couple of miles, perched uncomfortably on the edge of the road. I saw a church spire in the distance but the road dipped and it disappeared from view.

'Here we are,' said Adrien, stopping the car at the edge of a village.

'Where?'

'It's called Fore, a very interesting little spot.'

To me it looked like an ordinary Irish village, one straggly street. From where we now stood we could see right to the other end, and the general impression I got was one of an overall greyness. The house fronts were covered in grey plaster, the pavements and road were grey. There was no grass, no trees, no colour of any kind. I recognized the two pubs by the bicycles piled against their windows. Otherwise there was no sign that it might be inhabited. I remembered that Oliver Goldsmith had been born in this county but there was no hint of his romanticism in this bleak scene before me.

'Just my sort of town,' I said, gazing up at the peeling plaster on the small terrace we were passing.

'No – you must wait until we explore. Have you never heard of the Seven Wonders of Fore?'

I shook my head.

'It's a reference to St Fechin's miracles. He built a monastery here in A.D. 630 and if you look across there

104

you can see the ruins. They're the only authenticated Benedictine ruins in Ireland. Hermits were attracted to Fore in the eighteenth century because of its aura of holiness, and the big families – the Pakenhams and the Edgeworths – used to build cells for them. They thought that it used to add the finishing touch to their classical landscapes.'

I stopped listening, not because I was not interested in what Adrien said, but because I was so captivated by the desolation of the scene in front of me. The day was still and mild; there was no hint of blue in the sky. As we passed by the little windows with their obscuring lace curtains, I wondered about the lives of the people who sat behind them. How did you pass your time in a place like this? I could feel the weight of years, generations of apathy and dullness in the air around me. The utter hopelessness of such lives.

I could settle down here. I could spend my days in this sepia world.

Adrien was hurrying me along. 'There's a ninth-century church down here. The inscribed lintel stone is supposed to have been wafted from the monastery by St Fechin to its present position, that's one of the wonders.'

We entered through the arched doorway. The ruined stones seemed commonplace after the incorporeal ruin of the main street. I wandered after Adrien, kicking pebbles, letting his voice hum on. The thick stone walls had retained the winter cold and I shivered.

'Are you cold?' He swung round to look at me, then bent and kissed me on the mouth. I pushed him away – had he had a brainstorm? I moved to the doorway and out onto the road.

I was waiting for him at the car.

'I'm sorry. It's just that you looked so forlorn in there.'

There was nothing to say to that.

'You're not mad at me, are you?'

I thought – what am I doing with this foolish man? The fatuousness of his conversation seemed suddenly more than I could support. I longed for my kitchen and Henry.

'Let's go back.'

The rhythm of the car was soothing. I closed my eyes but opened them again as I thought of that awful kiss, those spongy lips leeching onto mine. I had been wrong to imagine that Adrien would view our outings as I did. I might see him as the chauffeur but he obviously had something else in mind.

'I won't go out with you again, Adrien, this is the last time.'

He jerked the car to a halt. 'For Christ's sake! Couldn't we discuss it when we get home?'

'There's nothing to discuss.'

'All right then.' He restarted the engine. 'It's a great fuss over nothing. I didn't think you were that sort of girl.'

I didn't care what sort of girl he thought I was.

'I mean – getting hysterical over a kiss.' Then, when I said nothing, 'I suppose you're sulking now.'

I concentrated on the road.

'That's it, you're sulking.'

'Look – I cannot stand your company for another second. If you don't shut up and drive me home, I'll jump out of the car.'

The violence of my reply seemed to shock him but he did as he was told. As he drew up outside the house, I thanked him for the drive. He nodded his head but said nothing. Before I had shut the car door he was revving up and, by the time I had my key in the lock, the hum of his engine had faded into the general traffic noise.

I was suddenly delighted that the outings were over. 'I'm home,' I called softly to Henry, realizing the truth of the phrase as I said it. I *was* home: this house was my home now and in the future. I was here to stay.

The world settled back. Adrien stayed away and Henry accepted his absence without comment. I went to work and returned. Together we cared for Mrs Harvey-

Brown, and in the evenings rested in the calm kitchen. Our days and nights took on a rhythm, stabilized into a tick-tock, tick-tock. We were like a married couple of long years' standing, living together, passionless, but with a memory of shared emotions. We had been through things.

There was a sweetness about our echoing lives, a grasping of the ethereal present for what it was, which I found comforting. I was pleased that there were no rings on the bell, that I could measure out beforehand my pleasure for the coming evening – cocoa, the warmth of a fire and bed. There was no longer any need to shy at shadows – my life was mapped out, my hours accountable. I could say where I would be, what I would be doing at any time of the day or week. This way I could shoal up and keep the terror out. It was only when life was on the move that there was any danger.

Under my care I watched Henry grow sleek. I washed his shirts and pressed his trousers. I fed him liver and porridge and home-baked bread. We listened to radio plays together and quiz programmes and shared the *Evening Mail*. If I had a fantasy, it was being married to him, a pleasing, bloodless relationship, only different from the present in its permanence. But it was a fantasy – I knew Henry would die of shock if I suggested marriage. There was something chaste about Henry – which is why I saw him as a suitable husband. But he would never view marriage in that light, his Protestant obtuseness and uprightness and integrity would prevent him. You had to be a Catholic or a Hindu to see things like that.

It was about two months after Adrien's last visit that Henry said, casually, one night, 'I wonder whatever has happened to Adrien, why he's stopped calling?' He was staring out the window so he didn't see my blush.

'I've no idea. He's probably just too busy. I mean, someone like that must have lots of friends and demands on their time.'

'Yes.' He didn't sound convinced.

107

'Anyway, I can't say I'm particularly missing him.'

'Aren't you? Still, it seems a pity.'

For some reason the conversation made me uneasy, for I had begun to believe that Henry had forgotten all about Adrien by now. And when I looked at him, the old puckers of anxiety were back round his eyes. He said no more then but the next evening he seemed ill-at-ease, jumpy. When we had finished our tea and as I was standing up to clear the table he said, 'Leave those, Ellen, I want to talk to you.'

I sat back, frightened by the seriousness of his tone.

He looked at me, then looked away. 'I've been wondering how I can tell you this.'

What, what?

'I had a letter from Mother's solicitors and I went in to see them yesterday. It's bad, Ellen, very bad. The house will have to go.'

'Go where?' I asked stupidly, unable to grasp what he was saying.

'I'll have to sell up, there's no other way.'

But there had to be another way. Everything just couldn't change like that overnight. 'Is it money?'

'Isn't it always?'

I rushed to my bedroom and came back with my Post Office Savings Book. 'Look Henry, here.' I thrust it into his lap. 'And I can give you more every week. I can give you everything except my bus fare. What do I need money for?'

But the book fell on the floor and he left it there unheeded. 'It's no good.'

'But you haven't even looked. Please, Henry –'

'My dear, don't make it worse. I need hundreds and hundreds of pounds. The house needs a new roof and Mother's investments are worth less and less all the time. Anyway, the doctor says at this stage that she really is beginning to need professional care. If I sold the house I could afford a private nursing home for her. I couldn't put her anywhere else, not on a long-term basis, she'd hate it. So you see, I have no choice.'

'But if the house is in such bad condition, you won't get anything for it anyway,' I said grasping at straws.

'You're wrong there. There's a lot of land and that's what will make it valuable, for building purposes. That's what they do with these old places, pull them down and build flats or offices in their place.'

I shook my head in disbelief. 'There must be something we can do – think, Henry. What about taking in more tenants, there are all those empty bedrooms and –'

'Ellen, dear, it's no good. I've gone into everything with the solicitors and it is the only possible way. If it wasn't for you I wouldn't care; I've never really liked this house. But I have been worried about what you would do.'

'Then you mustn't.' I could see that it was my turn to reassure him. 'You mustn't start worrying about me, I'll be fine. I've lots of choices.'

'That's why I was wondering about Adrien. I mean, I thought that you and he were –'

'No, Henry. Never.'

'It's just that he seemed so keen . . . it seemed somehow inevitable.'

'No, nothing like that. Will you excuse me, Henry, I'll just pop out for a breath of air and then I think I'll have an early night. I had a very busy time at the office today.'

I closed the back door behind me and stood leaning against the wall of the house. A wind stirred the scrawny leaves of the clematis and the stars shone down on the rough grass of our summer lawn. As I moved through the garden, my foot hit against something. I bent down and saw the meat-safe, abandoned there since last August. I felt the grossness of life around me, its energy pulling this way and that.

A rat scurried from my path, its eyes bright with terror. I listened to its frantic scrabblings in the undergrowth. Poor rat! Henry had laid poison earlier that day. I shivered, suddenly aware of the rawness of the night despite the gaudy prettiness of the stars. I turned back towards the house.

I slept, and awoke sometime before dawn. I felt

curiously calm as I wondered about what I must do. Outside, the birds had begun an intermittent chorus and I knew that soon Henry would awaken. I would lie and listen to the familiar sounds – the whine of bedsprings, the audible yawns and then the patter of feet past my door on the way to the bathroom. It was that presence which had sustained me through all the black nights. I knew he was there, next door, on the other side of the wall. I knew that if the horrors got too bad, if the ringing in my head became unbearable, I could go and scratch on his door, not necessarily to waken him, just to reassure myself that he was there. Then the death's-heads would recede and I could sustain another night.

But now I was on my own. I couldn't go back to my parents, a return to that state of innocence was lost for ever. And there was nowhere else to turn to. Unless of course . . . Henry's words of last night came back to me. Adrien. The memory of his pinkness filled me with distaste, his largeness, his schoolboy face. I thought of seeing him every morning at the breakfast table and of sharing a bed with him at night, his soft, plump hands straying round me. That's what marriage would mean – and worse.

There was another aspect however, and as I began to think of it, I could see that it might make the whole thing possible. By marrying Adrien, I would be forming a continuum with the past. If I had to leave this house and this street, if I were never to see the Harvey-Browns again, at least I would be sharing my life with someone who knew. Not everything, but enough. There would be the common memories, unarticulated probably, but there, between us. Every time I looked at him I would recall those days, that summer; and if I didn't love him, she had. The house would be pulled down. Mrs Harvey-Brown would die and Henry would disappear. Without Adrien my exile would be complete. I couldn't let that happen voluntarily.

And then there was the fact that I would never fall in love with Adrien. If I married him, he would be my fire

110

insurance. I was done with love, I had learned too late of its dangers and I didn't think, wounded as I was, that I *could* love again. But I could not be certain, and if Henry threw me out, God knows what flotsam I might cling to and with what eventual results. Distaste, which I would probably experience for the rest of my married life, seemed a small price to pay for such emotional security as life with Adrien would offer. I didn't have a choice.

I jumped out of bed, earlier for once than Henry. There were things to be done, plans to be executed if I was going to land my prize. The first problem would be making contact. I didn't think there was any point in inviting him round for tea – I would have to come upon him accidentally, as it were. Then I could suddenly become aware of his charms. I had no idea where he worked but I remembered him saying that he always parked his car in the same place, on the Quays, past McBirneys. It should be easy enough to spot, then all I had to do was hover until Adrien spotted *me*.

I hadn't the habit of looking in mirrors but now I stood squarely in front of the one on top of the chest of drawers. I would have to do something about my appearance, get my hair cut perhaps, and some clothes that fitted me. The prospect of such self-improvement afforded me no pleasure, but it might encourage Adrien and that was what I had to concentrate on now.

After breakfast I walked to the phone box on the corner and phoned Jack to tell him that I wasn't coming in that day. He didn't ask why and I didn't offer any explanation. Jack had such a high opinion of me and my dedication to the business that he would never suspect me of playing hookey. I caught the bus into town.

In Grafton Street I went into the first hairdresser's I saw.

'I want my hair cut,' I said to a girl standing behind a desk.

'Shampoo and restyle?'

'Just a cut.'

111

She looked at me as if I were slightly wanting. 'Have you an appointment?'

I shook the offending head.

'Then I'm afraid you'll have quite a wait – up to an hour.'

'I don't mind.'

She shrugged and beckoned me to follow her. 'You can wait here – I don't know when any of them can take you.' She pushed me into a chair and dumped some dog-eared magazines in my lap.

The air was hot and cloyingly scented and the long room seemed to be in a state of frenzy. Men and women rushed past with bottles and brushes in their hands, screaming to their colleagues at the far end of the shop. Women with red faces writhed under hairdriers that whined like spoilt children. I thought, I'd never come to such a place again whether or not I captured Adrien.

A man walked past, then turned to have another look at me.

'Who's doing your hair, love?'

'I don't know – anyone.'

He pushed my chin back with his forefinger. 'Quite a time since you've been.'

'You mean to a hairdresser's? I've never been before.'

'Wow!' It sounded admiring. 'I'll take you then – I like a challenge. Helen, kindly shampoo Madam.'

That curious liquidity of pleasure began to rise sap-like in my body as I looked at myself in the mirror of Switzer's Ladies Room. I was twenty pounds poorer and transformed. For the first time in my life I had breasts and a neck and a waist, and legs which seemed long and slim as I looked down at them. I touched my face and my newly lacquered hair, I stood on the points of my toes and stretched my arms. Then I collapsed in blushing confusion, turning my back on the glass, ashamed of my antics and my emotions. I reminded myself what little reason I had for self-liking as I tried to quell the warmth I had felt for the pretty girl in the glass. I faced her again, but this time it was to search for signs of imminent decay – the beginnings of a wrinkle, the greying of shining tooth enamel. I reminded myself of Mrs Harvey-Brown with her stink of mortality, our common stink. I reminded myself of the glum purpose behind all this titivation – the capture of Adrien.

Chastened, I grabbed my new handbag and set out for the Quays.

The Trinity College railings cast shadows and at first I thought it wasn't he – too coincidental that I should meet him like this, just as I was on my way to seek him out. But I knew the gait, and the overcoat, hung up – how many nights? – behind the studio door. Unprepared, I began to panic, but when I realized that he would pass by without seeing me, I reached out and touched his arm. He turned, blank-faced, then hostile, failing to recognize me.

'Hello, Adrien. How nice to bump into you like this.'

He stared. Then, 'Ellen!' His expression changed, as he looked, from curiosity to admiration. 'I hardly recognized you – you look a different girl.'

'And about time too,' I simpered. 'Adrien, I'd love to stay and chat, but I'm in a desperate hurry. I have to be back home by five and I'm looking for a taxi. You know what the buses are like.'

The rehearsed lie slipped smoothly out, a lucky invention I realized, watching his chest expand with self-importance as he began to take charge. 'I'll do better than that – I'll drive you home. No, I insist, the car's only five minutes away.'

It was all so easy, I felt cheated. He drove me home and I asked him in and Henry fell slobbering over him with delight. When would he call again? Oh, the next day, or the day after that, whatever suited. I answered his inquiring look in my direction with a flash of the eyes which said yes, Adrien.

'Don't mention about selling the house,' I said to Henry later that evening when he had gone home.

'Of course not, if you don't want me to.'

'I'd just rather he didn't know for the present.'

The next time he called I said boldly, 'Adrien, there's a picture on in town I'm dying to see,' and then nearly mucked it up when I couldn't think of the name of any film showing in Dublin that week.

After that, we began dating regularly, Wednesdays and Saturdays. We went for drives and walks and drank coffee in coffee houses and hotel lounges. I thought I could bear it, that I might even grow to like the outings, but by the third week I was in a state of twitching unease. It was not so much the dates themselves – I could support them – it was the anticipation before-hand. On Tuesday evenings and again on Fridays, I would begin to feel unsettled. My limbs could not compose themselves with any comfort and I wandered round the kitchen, even getting on Henry's nerves. Next morning, at the moment of awakening I would feel the weight of my head on the pillow and then I would count the minutes – every minute until I heard the little MG growling at the gate. Then things began to improve and I could start looking forward to my cocoa that night with Henry.

There were even aspects of Adrien's personality which I didn't find objectionable. He was good-tempered and he smelled nice and he made no demands on me. He talked too much for my liking, but at least what he said was impersonal. Early on I sensed, with relief, that he would not be the sort to look for emotional or spiritual intimacy. Physical yes, but that was something I felt I could handle. Infinitely easier to bare one's body than one's soul, and infinitely less embarrassing over toast and marmalade next morning.

I liked his cleanliness too. I came from a world where male hygiene was suspect, and it was nice to know that I wouldn't have to spend my life telling my husband to change his underpants. I could imagine wilder bases for a marriage.

The idea of marriage appealed to me. I saw a house

with walls, a fire to sit by, a blessed routine which would block out the shadows. I looked forward to a life of cleaning and cooking and ironing shirts – there was a solidity about it which I liked. It was the relationship which worried me.

I knew he existed – Adrien West, stockbroker – but I couldn't believe that he had anything to do with me. Being with him was like moving through a dream, bouncing along inside a chimera, not unpleasant but totally unreal. When we went to the pictures I often felt that what we saw on the screen held more substance than what was going on between the two of us. I listened incredulously to the conversations that the two of us engaged in as I felt, from inside, my features change from taut to stiff. It was disorientating; such a relief to get back to Henry at the end of it all.

But, of course, soon there would be no Henry to escape to, and although I was glad that there was no communication between Adrien and myself, no intimacy, I thought that there should be some point where we touched, if only tangentially. I had to get some sort of a hold on him, some perspective, before we got married. If we married as things stood, I could see myself losing whatever hold I had on reality.

Mother was right – there was something grotesque about it. And how could such a relationship be the foundation for the sort of domestic scenario that I had planned? I wanted my life to be ordinary, average, everyday, but every time I looked at my husband I must be jolted out of my secure and comfortable dullness. Every time I looked at his nice, decent, well-bred face, I must be reminded of the past.

'And how did you meet your husband?' was probably a fairly standard inquiry when young wives got together. Any answer I could give, even with the real truth concealed, would sound macabre.

But it would work because it had to work. There was no alternative. I'd have to shore it up, labour hard to give it an appearance of normality. And I could begin right away.

'Would you like to meet my parents?' I asked him, thinking of mother, the most solid, grounded entity in my world.

He seemed more embarrassed than glad. 'That sounds – very pleasant. Yes – why not, any time you like.'

Mother was equally accommodating – once I had advanced the truth a little.

'It's different if you're going to get married, that changes things of course.'

'But you *will* remember not to say anything, won't you?'

'What do you expect me to say? I'll welcome him, the same as I would anyone, and your father will too, but we're not going to start asking him about his intentions, if that's what's worrying you.'

'I just don't want any talk about marriage. We're not actually engaged, we just have this understanding but he's very shy about it.'

Or he might be if he knew.

'I'm not a fool, you know, Ellen. And anyway, you've never been exactly the soul of tact yourself.'

Seen from behind the windscreen of the MG, the neighbourhood seemed different, more lilliputian. There appeared to be fewer children about too, and more paint. Mother stood at the hall door, smiling.

'You're welcome, you're very welcome.' She pumped his hand up and down and beckoned me inside with a tilt of her head.

The front room was as I remembered it when there were visitors – too hot. The bottle of cream sherry on the sideboard was an innovation though: I never remembered drink in the house except at Christmas, and then it had been whiskey and port.

'Open the sherry, Tom,' mother commanded, still smiling, 'we'll have a drink before tea. Adrien – you don't mind if I call you Adrien? – I'm sure you could do with a bite to eat.'

116

In the kitchen the table was laid. There was ham and potato salad, brown bread, white bread, apple tart and fruit cake. There was the linen table cloth and the best china teapot. I felt a choking sadness as I thought of the weight on the little room of all the tea parties, all poor mother's wrong-headed efforts on my behalf. This was another one. Her attempts at gentility would not impress Adrien, he would probably find them pathetic. As for me, I was way past the stage where I wanted to impress.

'Eat up now and don't be shy. We've always had plenty to eat in this house. Even when times were lean, we never believed in stinting ourselves.'

Behind her back father winked at me. I turned away from him, and from the table, as I felt tears begin to irritate the back of my throat. That wink had wiped out the present and I was a girl again at home, with father offering his silent attacks against mother's excesses. I felt once more the raw misery of those days and, with it, the pulse of hope, which I hardly recognized but which kept on beating – there is a future out there, things will change. If I listened now I could hear silence, a silence which recognized the unchanging nature of the for-ever-after of my life.

'For goodness' sake, Ellen, you're dreaming again. Would you pay some attention to your guest and pass the apple tart.'

'Sorry.'

'Always the same, Adrien – Miss Head-In-Air I used to call her.'

Later, when, as mother put it, Adrien was washing his hands, she said to me: 'He's a very nice boy, Ellen, he really is. I take back all those things I said about him, I was overhasty in my judgement. Now that I've met him, I tell you, I couldn't have chosen better myself. And there's not a drop of the bigot in him, anyone can see that. I wouldn't be a bit surprised if he turned, do you know that? With good example from you, Ellen, that boy will surely turn.'

Like a pint of milk.

117

They both came to the car door to say goodbye. 'Now that you know us, just pop in any time, we'll always be glad to see you. You'll find we don't stand on ceremony but you'll be welcome nonetheless for that.'

'I like your parents,' Adrien said, as we drove back through an unexpected downpour.

'That's good.'

'I mean, they're awfully decent.'

I cleaned a circle for myself to look through the fogged-up window.

'They made me feel at home right away. And I think I got on all right with them. What did you think?'

'Oh, you did indeed.'

The next time he took me out, I could sense him feeling more anxious than usual. Several times he began to say something and each time changed his mind. Then, finally, it came out. 'Would you like to meet my mother? I'd like you to, if you wouldn't find it too much of a bore.'

'But, Adrien, there's no need for this tit-for-tat. Just because I asked you to meet my parents.'

'It's not that, really. I'd like you to meet her very much.'

The irony of it. The sought-after, ultimate prize falling like this into my ungrateful lap. How many evenings I had sighed on Myra's behalf as she had waited and hoped for such an invitation. It was enough to make you believe in God, or someone out there with a gibbous sense of humour.

'I didn't like to ask you before, I mean, I thought you might find it all very dull, but I would like you to meet her, and she's dying to meet you.'

'All right then.'

I looked at Adrien carefully. Used as I was to thinking of him as the casual young man who had lounged so large in the studio, I had failed to see him as he now was. But he was changed, totally changed. Deserted by his egotism, he had been transformed into a tentative,

118

highly-strung creature, jittery to please. I recognized his state and then cast it from me: he was in love.

It shouldn't have bothered me but it did. I wanted to be finished with all the messy pre-state, all the emotional slobbering. I wanted to be settled, anchored tidily in my little house where I could concentrate on the daily chores and make pretend that the outside world had finally gone away. But Adrien was the problem, not the outside world. If he weren't in love with me, he wouldn't marry me, and if he were in love with me, would I ever be free of his clamorous attentions?

I embarked on my trip to Greystones with no great enthusiasm.

It was a depressing journey, full of echoes. I hadn't visited Greystones since I was a child but it seemed unchanged, cosy and slightly shabby. I tried not to think of those conversations when it had been invested with such glamour, but a voice kept breaking through. 'It sounds wonderful, I know it must be marvellous. Ellen – I'm dying to be invited – I want that more than anything.'

I covered my ears with my fists and tried to concentrate on the houses we were passing.

'Headache?'

'Nothing much. Tension, I expect.'

The bungalow was perched on a headland, grey pebble-dash, looking down on grey sea. How aptly named the dismal place was.

Adrien unlocked the front door and I breathed the smell of ancient, ineradicable damp.

'My dears, how nice!'

The woman coming towards us with outstretched hands seemed smaller than the one I remembered from the inquest. She smelled of lavender but behind her glasses her eyes held the light of battle.

'Come into the sitting-room where it's warm.'

It was a small, cheerful room, an improvement on the dingy hall. There was chintzy furniture and standard lamps with pink shades. Everywhere there were framed photographs, mostly of a small boy and girl, sometimes with a bald man in the background. It was a careful room, careful and neat and cherished. The wood had been polished, as had the brass; the pretty rug in front of the fire had a careful darn in one corner. The paint was spanking new.

But what a sell-out – a suburban bungalow! Nothing at all like that house in Sligo, I was sure – what had it been called? Knaresborough? No decaying grandeur here, nor would it be tolerated. This room proclaimed itself middle class and proud of it. Which made sense, I suppose: in a land populated by peasants, the middle class had a certain cachet.

'Adrien, be a love and make the tea, the tray is all set in the larder. I want to have a little chat with – Ellen, isn't it?'

She settled me, with a cushion behind my back, and smiled at me reassuringly.

'I wanted Adrien to bring you to supper – or perhaps you call it tea? You must forgive any little *faux pas* until I get to know you better. I'm really hopeless at this sort of thing, I suppose it's because we've never mixed much. Even when Philip was alive,' – she bowed in the direction of one of the bigger photographs – 'we were inclined to stick to just old friends. I've always found it's so much easier with one's own sort. Oh dear!' She raised a lacy handkerchief to her lips. 'Have I done it again? Silly me! And I wouldn't mind, but really, I'm not at all like that. I mean, when Adrien was at Trinity, even then, there were plenty of –'

She broke off in confusion and began to poke at the fire with a long brass rod.

'Adrien tells me you're a city girl.'

'Yes.'

'Your parents aren't alive?'

'They are – both.'

'Oh good. Somehow I thought . . . I suppose because you live in a flat. But there we are!' She brightened. 'Just

120

another example of my fuddy-duddy ways. I would have found it very strange if Robin – Adrien's sister, you know – had gone to live in a flat. You must have very – enlightened parents.'

'They found it strange too.'

'Oh? Well. That's the way things are, isn't it? And do they get around, your parents I mean? Still active?'

'Yes.'

'That's nice for you and them. They must be fairly young then, not near retirement or anything?'

'No.'

'Splendid.'

'Father works for the Gas Company. He empties the meters.'

She blanched a little at this, then rallied. 'You seem a sensible girl, Ellen, and frank. I like that. I like Adrien to have a wide and varied circle of friends; even if I don't possess them myself, I think one should when one is young. Plenty of time for settling down later on – all his father's family took their time. You have to, you know, when you've got responsibilities. And I've always encouraged him to bring his friends home, I've kept open house here.' She glared around the room like a prison warder.

Adrien returned with the tea. If mother had erred on the side of abundance, Mrs West had gone to the other extreme. There was a pot of tea, cups and saucers and a plate with five pink and white iced biscuits. I wondered who was not going to have seconds.

Mrs West smiled at me as if I had passed some test. We sipped our tea and nibbled the biscuits. Adrien seemed determined to say nothing as he gazed out the window.

'Another cup, Ellen? Of course you will, and Adrien.'

'No thank you, Mumps. If you'll excuse me – there's just something.' And he backed away from the tea table.

Mumps. It didn't suit her.

'Would you care to see some family photos, I've got quite a collection. I think I've some of Adrien's

121

grandparents, the West grandparents that is. They came originally from Cavan, they lived in the one house in a place called Belturbet for five generations. Such a pretty house.'

I settled back to listen to the family history.

At first, I listened conscientiously. I nodded and smiled and shook my head in wonder. But after a while, I found myself falling into a trance-like state. The rise and fall of her voice, counterpointed by the rhythm of the sea down below, mesmerized me, and I could feel my eyelids beginning to close. I missed a question, failed to hide a yawn. By the time Adrien returned we were sitting in silence. I was overcome by weariness, scarcely able to lift my body from the settee, but as I raised my eyes to say good night to my hostess I noticed her expression of slightly puzzled offence.

'You seem to have quite an effect on us Wests.'

I kept my eyes on the road, watching it loom like some grey whale, then disappear as the cars approached and passed us.

'I've never seen her speechless before.'

'I suppose I wasn't much good. I'm hopeless at small talk. I'm sorry.'

And I was. I had been quite willing to be patronized by Mrs West, if only I could have sustained an interest.

Adrien laughed. 'Oh, she doesn't need any encouragement, you must have noticed that. But she's been a very good mother, to both of us, and it can't have been easy.' His voice had grown solemn. 'Do you know what age I was when my father died?'

'No.'

'I was nine. And Robin was only eleven. It may sound corny, but she devoted her life to us. I know she's a gas-bag and she has these illusions about the family. I think she sees us as minor nobility. But basically she's okay.'

'I'm sure she is.' I didn't know what else to say.

'She can be a bit of a bigot too – she's not overfond of RCs. I hope she said nothing – I mean, while I was out.'

'Oh no, not at all.'

'That's good anyway. She can sometimes make a bad impression, initially, but you'll find that basically she's very kind. She must have made a lot of sacrifices when I was at school and college but she's never allowed me to see it. She's always been frightfully decent to me. And it can't be easy, with Robin off in New Zealand. I mean – her grandchildren all born over there, she's never seen one of them. But she never complains.'

I had never heard Adrien speaking at such length. I could tell from the tone of his voice that he had more or less forgotten me, he was thinking aloud. His voice had softened as he spoke of her and I wondered about the love that existed between the steely little woman and her large, pink-washed son. Love between parents and children was not automatic – I knew that from my own circumstances – and there seemed little that was lovable about Mrs West. Yet it was clear that he did love her.

Perhaps that's why he was attracted to me – because I too gave so little in return. Perhaps in years to come I would listen to him explaining away my gruffness, telling unconvinced friends all about my heart of gold.

And now we were back where we started. I had visited his mother and he had met my parents and our relationship remained unchanged. Indeed, to such an extent unchanged that it could hardly be called a relationship at all. We were the two parallel lines, with nary a curve in sight.

Sometimes I asked myself what I was complaining about; wasn't this infinitely better than the other, the pawing and mauling which must surely result if a curve developed? Yes. But. At the rate we were going, we would never get past the polite and formal. In which case I could not see Adrien turning aside from the coffee cups some evening and addressing me; 'Pardon me, but would you care to marry me – that is, if you wouldn't find it too boring.'

\*    \*    \*

123

Henry was making me jittery. He had taken to looking at me slyly, when he thought I didn't see him. One night he asked me if I would mind if he started getting rid of some of the unwanted possessions of the house.

'I just want to start on it, Ellen, it's going to take such a time. Mother's always been an inveterate hoarder.'

'I'll give you a hand.'

'But there is no question of selling the house over your head – I don't want you to worry about that. I'll do nothing until I've seen you and Adrien off on your honeymoon.'

'That'll be the day.'

'What?' His eyebrows shot up in panic. 'Nothing wrong between you two, I hope?'

'No, Henry, just my little joke.'

'That's a relief.' The eyebrows returned to their normal position. 'Now, before I touch anything, I want you to choose something, some memento of the house.'

'I will, tomorrow, Henry.'

'There are some nice pictures in the drawing-room, Mother's always had a good eye. You know the little Yeats watercolour over the davenport, what do you think of that?'

But finally I chose a piece of Venetian glass that had sat on top of the mantelpiece in the drawing-room. It was a bauble, worthless but pretty. I liked the way it took in the light and held it at its heart. It, more than anything, would remind me of the studio.

Henry dismissed it. 'That's not up to much, just something that Mother picked up on her travels. Never mind. I'll choose something for both of you. It can be our wedding present to you from us.'

'I think you can't wait to get rid of me, Henry.'

'You know that's not true. There's no hurry, take all the time in the world . . .'

But he wasn't even trying to sound convincing. I suppose he wanted everything neatly settled before another winter set in, and I couldn't blame him. Adrien would have to be spurred on, brought to the sticking point.

But how?

I thought of direct seduction but balked at the image of that well-fed, well-exercised body. I was prepared to submit but I could not force myself to take the initiative.

Perhaps all we needed was a romantic setting. After all, I knew he was in love with me and presumably he wanted to marry me. Maybe all that was required was a more encouraging atmosphere.

'Adrien –' we were sitting beside one another in the front of the MG – 'have you ever been to a dance?'

'What a question to ask out of the blue.'

'Well, have you?'

'Years ago. I used to go fairly regularly when I was a student – talent spotting.'

For a moment he sounded like the young man who had lolled in the studio.

'Would you take me?'

'To a dance? But good heavens, Ellen, it doesn't sound a bit like you. What put dancing into your head, anyway?'

'Won't you take me, please.'

'Of course, if you're serious. It's just that you've never mentioned it before.'

He suggested a rugby club but I wanted something more romantic. I thought of the big dance hall in O'Connell Street. I had often passed by and it had seemed so special, with music spilling out onto the street and fluffy girls gathered expectantly in the foyer.

I wore my Switzer's dress and perfume. All day I practised looking sweet in front of a mirror and I reminded myself that all I had to do was keep saying yes.

But in spite of myself I was nervous. The air in the dance hall reminded me of that hairdresser's I had visited, too hot and scented, and the girls who stood in front of the long mirror in the Ladies seemed to be swallowing it in great gulps as they stared anxiously at their faces.

Adrien took my elbow. 'Are you ready then? I still think it was a crazy idea. I feel like somebody's grandfather.'

We butted our way onto the dance floor and it wasn't

until Adrien held out his arms that I realized in horror that I had never been on a dance floor before.

'I can't.'

'What?'

'I mean I never have. I can't dance.'

'There's nothing to it, just follow me.'

I shook my head. 'Let's watch for a while. I might get the hang of it if I just watch for a bit.'

We sat on a balcony and I listened to the music. The light was pinkish and dim and there were few people around. The music was muted and I thought, if he doesn't ask now, he never will. I settled my features in lines of encouragement and then realized that he probably couldn't see me anyway.

'Would you like a drink?' He sounded nervous, which I decided was probably a good sign.

'Yes please, anything you like.'

But when he came back with the drinks the atmosphere on the balcony had changed. The other tables had filled up and the orchestra had begun a fast number. The party at the next table were guffawing and swearing, already more than a little drunk, and I could see Adrien bristle. Perhaps the rugby club would have been a better choice.

'I'll have a go now,' I said as the music changed again.

It was easy. I simply shuffled round with Adrien as he guided me out of the path of other couples. Then I began to relax and feel the rhythm. Adrien's hand was firm in the small of my back. I was beginning to enjoy myself when the idiotic band leader turned smilingly to the dancers and announced, 'Something to liven things up.'

'Anyone can jive.' Adrien took me by the hand and flung me from him. I knew I was somehow, miraculously, to return to him, but I wasn't up to it. I went into a backward spin until I collapsed against something which at first seemed to be collapsing too. Then I found myself supported and a voice said, 'Steady on there, don't rush me off my feet.'

I turned. 'Sorry, excuse me.'

126

'A ladies excuse-me – delighted to oblige.'

He was smaller than I was and broad, with a smile that flashed gold. He grabbed me and sort of shunted me into the middle of the floor again. For a second I saw Adrien, standing with his mouth open, and I waved to him as I might to someone on a station platform.

'Aren't you the cheeky one though, asking this flower of Irish manhood up for a dance?'

My partner was smiling at me and bouncing up and down as if he were doing a jig at a feis. 'Come on now, girl, show a bit of jizz. Hop to it, that's right.'

Other couples had begun to give us plenty of room and I could understand their caution as I tried to avoid my partner's flying legs.

'That's it, loosen up there. That's why we Irish make such lousy dancers, too many inhibitions. You'd know my mother was Greek, wouldn't you?'

He bounced away from me and then returned, clapping his hands over his head. It seemed to me that everyone in the dance hall had begun to look at us.

'Another twirl, my dear?' he asked as the music stopped.

'No, thank you.'

'Ah well. You've probably had enough excitement for one night.' And he had slid through the wall of bodies on the edge of the dance floor.

I could tell from the set of his shoulders that Adrien was in a huff.

'I'm sorry, Adrien, but it really wasn't my fault. I –'

'You don't have to apologize. You have a perfect right to dance with whomever you please.'

'Oh Adrien!'

'Perhaps we should go downstairs. You'd have a better vantage point from there.'

The thought went through my head that he wouldn't be that easy to live with. He had a sulky mouth, which I had failed to notice up till now. 'Shall we dance?'

'As you please.' But he made no effort to move and wouldn't meet my gaze.

'Maybe we should go home?'

'It's entirely up to you.'

I couldn't take this. I wasn't capable of jollying him along, playing up to him until I had softened his mood. I didn't know how. But if I left things as they were, without offering some sort of apology to his wounded pride, I would be creating a situation.

'Would you –' I began. Then, 'Do you think we could –'

His eyes remained unblinkingly focused on a spot over my head.

'Let's get married.'

I suppose I blurted it out like that because that was what I had been thinking about all evening. But I shut my eyes now so as not to see his reaction.

Nothing happened. If I opened them, I thought, perhaps I'll find that he's walked away. Then, as I was about to, I felt his hand drop onto mine.

'You're an odd sort of girl.'

That was all he said.

So it was done.

'Let's get out of this ghastly place and celebrate.'

'Let's go home and tell Henry.'

'I must phone Mother first.'

'I'm sorry we can't tell my parents too.'

'Why not? It's not every day their daughter gets engaged. We'll call on old Henry first, then it's off to see them.'

We spent the next few hours rushing around. As we said good night to Henry, we saw a light on in Mrs Earley's sitting-room, so we called in to tell her too. Everywhere we went people kept regretting their lack of alcohol. 'If only we'd known, we'd have had a bottle opened.' But I needed no alcohol, I was euphoric on happiness. This is me, this is it, I said to myself, normal, ordinary and about to begin to live happily ever after.

'We'll look for a ring tomorrow,' Adrien said as he kissed me good night.

The kiss tasted of gratitude rather than passion and

didn't offend me as the other one had.

'I don't really want a ring.'

'But you've got such pretty hands.'

I didn't mind that either and I went to bed with a growing confidence in myself. Marriage to Adrien wouldn't only be a refuge from the world but a more positive experience, offering new and unthought-of pleasures. Before I drew on my nightdress, I stood in front of the wardrobe mirror and looked at my naked body. I almost laughed out loud, it looked so cherished, so well tended. The skin covered the bones without a pucker anywhere; the pinkness of my nipples surprised me and the round swell of my belly. I wondered at how it had bloomed, secretly, in spite of everything. It was untouched, perfect, and, finally, with a purpose. I wished I was married now, this minute, so that Adrien could see me as I saw myself.

But happiness is dangerous. When you are happy you let your guard down, you forget the dangers that beset you, you forget the caution of a lifetime.

I woke early next morning. The moment of awakening is always full of peril anyway, and this time I was swamped by the sensuousness of the occasion. I felt my body at ease, savoured the delicious warmth which it had generated during the night, and I pulled my bedclothes in to secure my cocoon. I yawned and scratched my head, my thoughts wandering, idling here and there.

Tinny tick-tock, otherwise nothing stirring. An hour at least till Henry groaned, then padded past the door. This bed groaned too when I turned. Glad to be out of that on a well-sprung mattress. Large, of course – connubial. Mother had always complained of her mattress, said it sank in the middle so that no matter how she tried, how far she put between herself and father, they always woke up on top of each other. Mrs West had praised twin beds, more hygienic, and she was speaking disinterestedly, from a scientific viewpoint. And heat,

heat and weight, they might prove contentious. Closed windows, lots of blankets, even in summer. Blankets spelled security, although with a husband that might be different. That made me blush, that word, and I thought I had stopped blushing. How I had sought a cure for that. In books it was supposed to be becoming, comely maidens did it. But they didn't blush like me, not with that ugly red stain, extending even down to the chest. Myra had said, 'You shouldn't try to cure it, Ellen, you should learn to do it prettily.' As she did. Hardly noticeable anyway, with those rosy cheeks, just a suggestion . . .

The nausea came from my chest, not my stomach, biley and bitter. I rose and threw a towel over the wardrobe mirror, blushing now in shame as I remembered last night. How could I have forgotten myself so far, forgotten my circumstances? Now I knew there was something monstrous in my make-up. I had no right to pursue a normal life, but if I even had the inclination, then I was evil. I had destroyed a life, three lives really, for surely Dr and Mrs Boland's were destroyed too. Yet here I was, touching my white skin with pleasure, thinking of a future with hope. Forgive me, I said to the empty room, forgive me.

By the time I had prepared breakfast and had Mrs Harvey-Brown's tray ready, the familiar greyness had settled back around me and I realized that my reactions last night had been an aberration. My despair hadn't deserted me, it had merely seemed to in the momentary excitement. This morning I viewed my engagement to Adrien as satisfactory, no more. I would have a roof over my head and a presence against the dark.

Of course, no one else saw it like that. Chased from the house by Henry's coyness, I reached the office early only to find nice, taciturn Jack in a state of some agitation.

'You'll be wanting time off this morning.'

Seeing my blank face he continued, 'On account of the ring. Mr West rang me.'

Curse Adrien.

Jack followed me to my coat-hanger and back to my seat. He stood there as I took the cover off the type-writer.

'I want to tell you something.'

'Yes. The accounts are nearly ready for last month –'

'Leave them. It's advice I want to give you. I never interfere, I never talk out of turn, but I'm advising you now, don't go into rented accommodation. That was the downfall of Mrs Taylor and me and it took us years to recover from it. Now, I don't offer advice but I know a man, I learned the hard way and if you and Mr West will just have a chat with me when he comes in I can give you this man's address and he's the very man to settle all your problems housewise.'

'Thank you.'

'I hope you don't think I'm talking out of turn, but it's on account of what me and Mrs Taylor suffered. I wouldn't like to see you go through the same thing.'

The phone on my desk rang and I turned to it with relief. But it was mother.

'And how are you feeling this morning?'

'Fine.'

'I must say you are a cool one. Ellen, I want you to come over this evening, we'll have to start thinking about the trousseau.'

'I don't want one.'

'But that's not the point, you have to have one. Other-wise you wouldn't be properly married.'

'Anyway, I can't afford one, I've other things to spend my bit of money on. You hardly expect Adrien to buy it for me, do you?'

'You can be so silly sometimes,' mother answered crossly. 'Of course Adrien wouldn't be expected to pay for anything – what an idea! You seem to forget that *we* might have some money. Daddy and I aren't exactly pau-pers and you are our only child, after all.'

I thought of all the years of saving: twenty-five watt bulbs in the hall, spirals of newspapers to save the matches and, shame of my adolescence, home-made sanitary towels. And now all those painfully collected pennies were to be frittered away on lacy underwear.

In the afternoon, Mrs West rang. 'It's wonderful news, dear – I'm so glad. Now, I want you to come over and see me, on your own, we don't want Adrien. I've got some silver, nothing very fancy, just bits and pieces, but I want you to take what you will.'

'That's very kind of you Mrs West but –'

'No buts. Come to lunch. We can have fun going through everything.'

Fun, in that creaking bungalow, poised to topple into the sea.

'Let Adrien decide.'

'Absolutely not. He has no interest and, anyway, you will be mistress of your home. It's your concern, my dear, not his.'

On the bus, on the way home from work, I stared at the ring on my finger. Dully, the diamond stared back at me, unimpressive in the yellow light.

'We'll have to start looking at houses soon,' Adrien had said, holding my hand in the Shelbourne bar. 'Have you any idea where you'd like to live, or what kind of house? It's up to you, darling, I don't really mind. Anywhere, as long as it's accessible. We want our friends to be able to come and visit us.'

I thrust my hand into my coat pocket as resentment against Henry suddenly flooded through me. He had, through his mismanagement, brought all this on top of me. He should have seen to the roof sooner, stopped things from falling apart while he still could. And I would have looked after him and helped with his mother. I would have made him cocoa on cold nights and kept the fire burning brightly in the range. Later on, when he grew older, I would have tended him and the house, my tenderness increasing in pace with their fragility. I would have kept the world at bay. Instead of which I was facing a life with Adrien full of brightness and smartness and dinner parties with young married

132

couples. And it was all Henry's fault.

The following evening, I went home. Mother, looking ten years younger, took me into the sitting-room.

'What's wrong with the kitchen?'

'There are times and places,' was the mysterious reply.

'Where's Father?'

'Getting a cup of tea for us, it'll be a long evening, with all we've got to discuss. You'll be married in white of course.'

'Will I?'

'Unless you know some reason why you shouldn't.'

None. Red might be a more suitable colour but I was definitely entitled to march up the aisle in white, an intact virgin.

'And you'll be married from home, properly, in the parish church where you were baptized. Oho, Ellen, this will be a wedding to remember. And who would have thought,' she smiled and shook her head, 'that things would turn out so well. Why, even if you'd gone to the university you couldn't have done any better for yourself.'

But the following day at work she rang me up in a terrible state. Apparently the parish priest was not as enthusiastic about my forthcoming wedding as she was. He explained to her that, as I was marrying a heretic, it should be done as discreetly as possible, so as not to encourage the others, I suppose. So it would be a side altar, with a minimum of fuss.

'Some hole-in-the-corner affair, that's what he's really suggesting and I won't have it, not for my only child. I said to him, "The boy's a Christian after all. It's not as if she was marrying a Mohammedan or a Jew." But he seems to lump them all in together.'

'That's it then – we don't seem to have any choice.'

'Don't we though! There are other priests around. And other churches too. For two pins I'd –'

But the pips went and I didn't hear what she'd do.

The wedding pursued me in my dreams, most cruelly in this one which recurred. I was in the middle of preparations, in a sea of tissue paper and hysteria. My panic started to grow, I could feel it begin to choke me, and I felt that I could not survive another minute when, blessed realization, I awoke in my dream to the knowledge that there was no wedding. I hadn't seen Adrien for months and I was living in a state of quiet happiness with Henry. Usually at this point, I awoke out of my dream, but for several seconds the sense of well-being persisted. I lay, searching for the source of my happiness, savouring the novelty of the feeling and then some sound – a bird note from the garden, a sighing explosion of wind against the door – tore through my confusion and I was faced with two neatly sorted piles: dreams and reality.

It seemed now as if all stillness had gone from my life. I was constantly being whizzed round various suburbs in Adrien's little car or walked round city shops by mother. There were decisions I had to take, choices I had to make, advice I had to listen to, and all this that I might thereafter retire from the human race. I had to keep this goal in view or I could not have endured another smiling second. I had discovered that, if I smiled, they at least stopped asking me how I was, so I smiled and smiled until my jaws ached.

One afternoon, when we had tramped through every single department in Clery's, even the sportswear, mother said, 'Let's have a cup of tea in the restaurant. My feet are killing me.'

She scolded the waitress for the slovenly appearance of the table and settled her parcels round her. Then she turned to me, beckoning me closer to her. 'I couldn't bring this up at home, not with Daddy around.'

'What?'

'I just wondered, it has to be gone into . . . Do you know all about that side of marriage, Ellen?'

'What side?'

'Now you're trying to annoy me. I'm your mother and I have to ask these things, it's my duty. Now, all I'll say is –'

'I know all about it, Mother, you don't have to tell me.'

'Nevertheless, I'm going to.' She sighed and looked at me, her mouth drooping mournfully. 'Maybe women differ but I've never enjoyed that side of marriage. And I'm quite sure you won't either. But you have a duty, Ellen, you have to obey your husband in that respect, even if you don't like it much. That's why marriage is more of a sacrifice for women, but then they have the children and that makes up for it. And anyway,' she added after a pause, 'they say that Protestant men have more self-control in that respect. I don't know why that should be, but I've often heard it said by them that should know. Funny, isn't it?'

'Inbreeding, I'd say.'

She nodded with complete seriousness. 'You could well be right.'

Adrien was showing no signs of wanting to ravish me but this was not due to his Protestant self-control, I believed, but rather to his state of being helplessly in love. Love had changed him, taking away his old bounce and assurance, and although I liked the new Adrien better, I could see that to the outside world he must seem a poor thing. He beseeched me with his eyes and sought to appease me with his smiles. He was incomplete, ego-less, looking out on the world with hesitation, without dash, without style. So must Myra have seemed to him. And I to Myra?

I wondered at the perversity of love. Did Adrien's passion grow as he became more aware of my indifference towards him? And if I should suddenly fall in love with him, would I as suddenly see him reflate, like a pink balloon, as his voice increased by several decibels? Then he would fill his tweeds with that assurance that I remembered so well and treat me with the good-natured contempt that he had had for me in the past.

How pleased I was to be finished with love.

But, though I had no affection for Adrien, I could see that there was a bargain to be kept. He would provide me with a shelter so I must endeavour to provide him with whatever

135

it was he needed in a wife. I was determined to play fair, and it must grow easier as, living together, he grew used to me and became less obsessed. I might even be able to revive his interest in cricket.

It was mother who reminded me of cricket. She had summoned me to Sunday dinner but when I arrived there were no smells of cooking and the kitchen was empty.

'Up here,' she called and I climbed the little staircase to her bedroom.

'Sit down,' she patted the bed, making room for me beside her. I looked around me – it was unchanged from my earliest memories. There was the bed we had sat in with its carved mahogany headboard; the pictures on the walls, fading prints of the Annunciation, Crucifixion and Resurrection; there was even the same smell, recognized immediately, a mixture of beeswax and camphor. I had spent many summer afternoons here, fingering with pleasure my mother's frugal stock of cosmetics, wishing for the day when I would have my own.

'You know, Ellen, it really is a pity you were never more interested in sport.'

I waited, speculating on what had prompted this.

'I did try, I even bought you a tennis racket, if you remember, but somehow you just never got keen. And it would be so useful now.'

'Why now?'

'When you're married, I mean. A woman needs to have her own interests and with Adrien so keen on cricket –'

'Who told you that?'

'His mother, of course. She was telling me about all the trophies he won at school and –'

'But when were you talking to Mrs West?'

'I don't know why you should take that tone, Ellen, as if there was something wrong in what I've done. Naturally, when I got her letter, I thought I'd ring up and thank her and all that.'

'She wrote to you?'

136

This was becoming more inexplicable every second.

'With the invitation. And that reminds me – which do you think I should wear, the black or the purple?'

She was poking her head in the wardrobe and waves of camphor wafting from it were causing my eyes to water.

'I like the purple, it's so rich, but then again, black is safer. I mean, you can't go wrong with black, at my age anyway.'

'Mother, where are you going?'

'Hasn't Adrien told you?'

'Told me what?'

'We're all going to the Gresham!' Her neck grew red with pleasure. 'I've had a very nice letter from Mrs West inviting Daddy and me to meet her. She suggested a drink in the Gresham, and she did sound nice on the phone when I rang up to thank her, I thought that'd be better than writing, give her more time. And I've sent Daddy's good suit to the cleaners so that's taken care of everything if I could just decide on which dress. Now, Ellen, tell me the truth, is the purple a bit much?'

I shook my head. 'But, I mean, why does she want to meet you?'

'I sometimes wonder where I got you from. Of course we must meet – we're going to be part of the one family from now on. It wouldn't do to have us introducing ourselves at the church door – now, would it?'

I just stared as she pranced in front of the mirror.

'She says that we are to be her guests, that she won't hear of it any other way. But if she won't let Daddy pay for anything, then I've decided I'll send her a nice bouquet of flowers afterwards. That'd be the correct thing to do in the circumstances. And I've decided finally on the black. It's more elegant somehow.'

Mrs West had decided on black also, and with the men's dark suits we must have looked like a funeral party as we stood on the steps of the Gresham.

'So good of you to come,' said Mrs West, taking

father's arm and sweeping him in through the door.

With no more than a moment's hesitation, mother grabbed Adrien. I trailed along behind.

'Isn't this lovely!' Mother beamed round. 'A very nice hotel.'

'It's a family tradition, coming here when we have something to celebrate. My father used to bring us here as children every year at Christmas week. We'd do our shopping in Switzer's and then the car would be waiting to take us to tea at the Gresham. How we used to look forward to it.'

Suitably silenced by this reminder of past grandeur, I wondered what she planned to offer us this evening, not tea anyway, not the right time.

'And I thought this was the place to meet to celebrate our children's happiness.'

Mother cleared her throat. 'Funny things, traditions. Now, in our family, we always liked to celebrate at home. I remember my mother saying that, no matter how big the crowd, she liked her celebrations to be home-based.'

I had visions of a marquee rising up in granny's back yard.

'How interesting,' said Mrs West, without inflection.

'Of course, it's all a question of taste and families differ. And I will say, this is very nice.' Mother was determined to be fair.

But Mrs West won the next round. A waiter, an elderly man, glided towards us and bowed deeply in front of Mrs West. 'Good evening, Ma'am. Everything is in readiness.'

'Splendid, William. Everyone's here.'

William summoned an underling, a youngster of about forty, who placed a long-stemmed shining glass before each of us. Then, reaching up towards William, he placed a large green bottle in his hands. William in turn placed it in front of Mrs West.

'Yes, William, that's fine. You just go ahead and open it.' She smiled at us in turn. 'I hope everyone can drink

138

champagne – I thought this was an occasion for it.'

Mother nodded her head in approval. 'I do like a drop of champagne.'

I had never tasted it in my life and I couldn't imagine that she had either. It saddened me to think that she hadn't; or that she couldn't look back on a childhood studded with afternoon teas at the Gresham. I stretched over and squeezed her hand under the table.

'We're rather fond of champagne in our family,' I said. 'You could call it a family weakness.'

Mrs West proposed the toast. I took a sip and then another, enjoying the way in which the wine rasped the back of my throat. Its coldness sent a shudder through my body.

The waiter poured some more of the fizzy liquid into my glass.

'It's quite potent,' Mrs West warned.

'Never mind,' Adrien put an arm round my shoulder and left it there. 'I'll look after her, and anyway, I'm doing the driving.'

Perhaps it was the wine, but I suddenly began to feel very removed from the scene around me. The life of the hotel surged and I could hear a whole variety of sounds, but they came to me as if from a distance. A blond cherub passed by, calling out for a Mr Williamson; a bell sounded somewhere, and someone laughed.

Our little group was becoming more animated. I watched their mouths opening and closing, without listening to the sense of what they said. Their cheeks were uniformly rosy and their eyes sparkled. Father looked more lively than I had seen him for years. He reminded me of Mr Punch.

But what was I doing here? I was too old for puppet shows, and besides, I had seen this one too often. And if I didn't escape pretty sharp, I would find myself on stage too.

I stood up from the table, ignoring the startled faces turned towards me. I couldn't go through with it – I didn't know why I had ever imagined that I could. And now I must disappear before someone tried to dissuade me. The street was no good, I would surely be pursued. But the lift caught my eye, waiting like a gilded birdcage. I got in and pressed a button at random.

The silence was total. The thick carpet muffled all sounds and the dim wall lights showed me a corridor, apparently endless and deserted. I walked past doors until I came to one marked Bathroom. I paused; nothing stirred. I went inside and turned the key.

The bath was huge and shining, the walls reflected back at me their pink tiled surface. A white chair was drawn up before a dressing table, laid with cut glass dishes of talcum powder with giant pink puffs. It was hard to breathe in the stale, scented air and as I looked around me I experienced the same feeling of unreality that I felt when I thought about my future life.

I looked at my face in the mirror. It was no longer familiar to me. It wasn't the face that I had tried for so long to make something of, that I had wept over as I examined it in my little bedroom mirror. It was a blank face, giving nothing much away. Like those improbable faces of mannequins that you see in the pages of fashion magazines. Idly I dipped the puff into the dish of powder and patted it over my face. I did it again, this time closing my eyes. I looked once more. I pulled back my hair and stared ... White and still, like the glare of a noonday sun in a dead landscape. Or like a corpse, waiting to be shovelled into the ground. One day I would look like this, without the aid of powder.

And that surely was the justification for the continuation of my life: the sure approach, no matter how slow, of my death.

With my handkerchief I began to scrub at the powder on my face. I recalled a scene from last summer. Lying on the grass, I had been bitten by something.

'I'm sure it was an ant,' Henry had said. 'Let's just see.'

Then he cut up an orange and placed a piece on the

grass. As we watched the ants began to gather. Soon there were hundreds of them. The flesh of the orange changed to black as the bodies covered it completely. Their frantic energy mesmerized me and, although I looked and looked, I could find no purpose to their labour.

'It's an infestation,' Henry had said and, raising a kettle high in the air, he poured a stream of boiling water down on top of them, round and round in circles while the water remained.

And there was some consolation, on top of justification; there was something to ease the burden of guilt. That guilt had been induced by feelings of self-importance, but these feelings were false, all false. All I had to do was to convince myself of the purposelessness, of which I was a part, and my nights could be quiet, my days tolerable.

I combed my hair and stood up. All traces of powder were gone from my face and the mask was in place again. I would put an end to my fussing. I would walk out, down those stairs, and with each step I took I would whisper: I will, I won't. When I reached the bottom step, it would be either yes or no and I would go to join Adrien or turn my back on him.

And, like the rest of my life, it had nothing to do with me.


THE END